Jack was watching her.

Toni felt him cover her hand with one of his, and drew comfort from his nearness. At that moment, in the sweltering heat, she felt she would be prepared to lie beside this man and slip quietly into oblivion. . . On the other hand, it might be rather nice if he were to make love to her first. . . She felt a smile touch her lips at the thought. Was she starting to hallucinate?

GW00375138

Dear Reader

In Australia, Marion Lennox has Nikki and Luke find a STORM HAVEN; Laura MacDonald's Toni finds herself IN AT THE DEEP END with her new boss in Africa; at the health centre, Margaret O'Neill's Dr Ben Masters becomes NO LONGER A STRANGER to Clare Lucas; and we meet Michael Knight again—first seen in PRIDE'S FALL—in Flora Sinclair's KNIGHT'S MOVE as he meets his match in Jessica Balfour. Happy New Year!

The Editor

!!!STOP PRESS!!! If you enjoy reading these medical books, have you ever thought of writing one? We are always looking for new writers for LOVE ON CALL, and want to hear from you. Send for the guidelines, with SAE, and start writing!

Laura MacDonald lives in the Isle of Wight. She is married and has a grown-up family. She has enjoyed writing fiction since she was a child, but for several years she worked for members of the medical profession, both in pharmacy and in general practice. Her daughter is a nurse and has helped with the research for Laura's medical stories.

Recent titles by the same author:

STRICTLY PROFESSIONAL
TO LOVE AGAIN

IN AT THE DEEP END

BY

LAURA MACDONALD

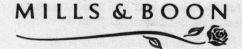

MILLS & BOON

MILLS & BOON LIMITED
ETON HOUSE, 18-24 PARADISE ROAD
RICHMOND, SURREY TW9 1SR

*MILLS & BOON, the Rose Device and LOVE ON CALL
are trademarks of the publisher.*

*First published in Great Britain 1994
by Mills & Boon Limited*

© Laura MacDonald 1994

*Australian copyright 1994   Philippine copyright 1995
This edition 1995*

ISBN 0 263 78916 0

*Set in Times 10 on 12 pt. by
Rowland Phototypesetting Limited
Bury St Edmunds, Suffolk*

03-9501-42489

Made and printed in Great Britain

CHAPTER ONE

So THIS is Africa! Toni Nash stepped on to the tarmac at Nairobi Airport and felt as if she had entered some giant oven. Together with her fellow passengers she made her way past heavily armed guards to the main terminal buildings to clear Customs, collect her luggage and find the coach that would take her to the Jacaranda Hotel.

If it was possible, it was even hotter on board the coach, as it had none of the air-conditioning of the British Airways flight, and within minutes the cotton shirt Toni was wearing was sticking to her back. It was late afternoon in mid-October, but anything less like autumn it was difficult to imagine as the coach hurtled through the dusty streets of Nairobi, its gears grinding noisily, its tyres squealing.

Here the heat seemed to settle like a pall and poverty and wealth vied for supremacy; large modern buildings of marble, concrete and glass soared from tree-lined avenues into the white hot sky but on every street corner groups of vagrants could be seen openly begging, and behind the modern façades Toni caught glimpses of a warren of back streets and shanty-style buildings. She was uncertain what she had been expecting but she had no time for further speculation, for the coach drew up at the hotel and amid the hustle and bustle of the crowds who thronged the street a smiling black doorman in green and gold livery came forward to greet them, and a group of boys began squabbling over luggage.

The hotel lived up to its name: a long, low, white building, it was surrounded by jacaranda trees, palms, and brightly coloured flowering shrubs that filled the air with a sweet, faintly cloying scent. The hotel entrance was at the top of a short flight of steps beneath a striped awning that matched the doorman's livery and opened through revolving glass doors into a cool, spacious, dimly lit foyer.

Toni checked in at the desk then, as the young Kenyan receptionist handed her the keys to her room, she paused.

'Could you tell me, please, is Dr Jack Christy in the hotel?' she asked.

The girl glanced at the board behind her, nodded, then, leaning forward across the desk, said, 'I believe Dr Christy is in the bar.'

Toni was about to say she would go to her room first, to freshen up before she met her new boss, but curiosity suddenly got the better of her and she glanced over her shoulder, following the girl's gaze. From where she was standing, through an archway at the end of the foyer, she could see directly into the hotel lounge. A couple were standing at the bar.

The man was dressed in typical safari gear: pale-coloured trousers and shirt. He was tall, loose-limbed but muscular, his skin weathered and tanned from years spent in the hot sun. His tawny-coloured hair swept back from a widow's peak and when he turned towards her she saw that his features were sharp, the nose high-bridged, curved, the jawline firm, the mouth hard and arrogant, but his eyes, as they met hers were as grey as an English, winter sky. Toni's immediate impression was of a bird of prey, but intuition told her he was the man she was looking for.

'I'll go to my room in a moment,' she told the receptionist and, leaving her luggage to the boys, she walked slowly into the lounge.

The woman at the man's side had her arm possessively through his. She was also tall, a voluptuous brunette, the simplicity of her olive-green safari dress a perfect foil for her exotic dark beauty.

As she approached, Toni suddenly felt tiny, pale and insignificant beside this dramatic-looking couple. She gritted her teeth and stepped forward—it had to be done, she had to introduce herself; there was no one else to do it.

'Dr Christy?' she asked.

He had half turned away from her but at the sound of his name he glanced back. Then he nodded, the grey eyes wary, instinctively narrowing.

'Hello.' She held out her hand, aware that the dark-haired woman was eyeing her up and down in the way she might eye something objectionable. 'I'm Toni Nash—your new assistant.'

Silence followed her statement, a silence in which she saw surprise flicker across the man's hard features, to be immediately replaced by a deepening frown.

'You're Dr Nash!'

It was almost an accusation and she flinched at the lack of warmth, the absence of welcome.

'Yes.' She nodded and took a deep breath. 'I've just

arrived——' she began, but he cut her short.

'You're Dr Tony Nash?'

'Yes. . .'

'What damn fool sort of a name is that for a woman—Tony?'

She blinked at the harshness of his tone. 'My name is Antoinette,' she replied tightly taking a deep breath, 'but that's a bit of a mouthful, so people call me Toni——'

'I was expecting a male assistant,' he interrupted rudely.

His companion lifted a beautifully manicured hand to hide a smile. 'Looks as if you've been landed again, Jack,' she murmured.

Indignantly Toni glared at him. 'I can assure you, Dr Christy,' she began, 'I am every bit as qualified as any male doctor and I've had experience in——'

'I don't doubt it,' he said abruptly, turning back to the bar, lifting his pint glass and taking a long drink, finishing the contents. 'They all say that,' he added as he set his glass down again.

'All. . .?' She frowned.

'The other females they've sent me.' He replied without turning, staring moodily into the dregs at the bottom of his glass.

'You mean. . .?'

'Oh, yes——' he looked over his shoulder at her then '—at least three—all well qualified, all experienced, all enthusiastic.' His tone was heavy with sarcasm.

'Then what. . .?' She looked bewildered. 'I don't understand.'

'Not one of them had the stamina necessary to

sustain life in the Tanzanian bush for any length of time.' He leaned back against the bar and stared coolly at her, his gaze taking in her small-boned frame, her gamine features, the short blonde hair, its wispy tendrils cut urchin-style.

'And I can't imagine you will be any different,' he said at last.

'Then I shall just have to prove otherwise, won't I?' She glanced from Jack Christy to his companion then back again, keeping her tone light but inside seething at his attitude and dismayed at the prospect at working in close proximity to such a man.

'Hah! I give you a month—if that!' With an impatient gesture he turned back to the bar.

Furiously Toni glared at his unyielding back, opened her mouth to say more, caught sight of the woman's faintly condescending smile, thought better of it, turned abruptly away and marched back to Reception.

At the sound of a knock on the door of her hotel bedroom Toni turned from the wardrobe and hurried across the room. 'Who is it?' she called through the door, cautious as to the identity of the caller.

'Hilary Moss—I'm with a team from the charity WaterAid—I understand we're travelling down to Tanzania together.'

She tugged open the door and found herself face to face with a stocky, fresh-faced woman of about thirty.

'Dr Nash, I presume?' Hilary Moss grinned, her face lighting up.

'Please—Toni.' She held out her hand, which was immediately gripped in a firm handshake. 'Come in.'

She stood aside and the woman came into the room.

'When did you arrive?' Hilary perched on the edge of the bed and glanced round the room, then, not giving Toni a chance to answer, went on, 'I say, this room is much bigger than ours—I'm sharing with Ruth Galloway—another member of our team,' she explained.

'I got here this afternoon,' said Toni.

'Ah, we've been here since yesterday,' said Hilary, 'been exploring Nairobi, at least some of us have—Ruth took to her bed after the flight and hasn't been seen since.' She grimaced. 'There are four of us,' she added as an afterthought, 'myself and Ruth and the two men—Paul Davis, a conservation expert and Henry Bowyer—he's an engineer with the water industry.' She paused and looked reflectively at Toni who had perched on the edge of a cane ottoman. 'I understand you are with the voluntary service and are joining Jack Christy? Have you met him yet?'

Toni was unable to prevent herself pulling a face at the sound of Jack Christy's name.

'I see you have.' Hilary chuckled. 'Quite a character, isn't he? Reminded me of the original white hunter with that tanned skin and bleached hair. . .attractive, in a rugged sort of way. . .' she mused.

'If you like that sort of thing,' retorted Toni briskly.

'Which you quite obviously don't.' Hilary grinned again then, growing serious, narrowed her eyes and surveyed Toni. 'You married?'

'Good heavens, no. I'd hardly be volunteering to disappear into darkest Tanzania if I were.'

'Oh, I don't know. . .people do. . .'

'There can't be too many spouses prepared to put up with that.' She gave a short laugh.

'What about the beautiful Shakira? Have you met her yet? She seems to put up with Jack Christy's absences—mind you, I don't mind betting the reunions between those two must sizzle when they do get together after being apart for so long.'

At Hilary's words Toni glanced up sharply. 'They're married, those two?' A mental picture of the dark-haired woman's red-varnished nails on Jack Christy's arm came into her mind.

'Almost.' Hilary shrugged. 'Engaged, I believe. . . or so one of the bar staff told Paul. How do you feel about working with Jack Christy?'

'I don't know. I was looking forward to it. . . I've heard stories about his work in the bush stations. . . but now. . .' She trailed off.

'Now you've met him, you're not sure, is that it?'

'Something like that, yes; he's not what I expected and he wasn't exactly happy to meet me. . .'

'What do you mean?' Hilary frowned. 'Wasn't he expecting you?'

'Yes. . .I mean no.' Toni laughed when she saw Hilary's expression. 'What I really mean is that he was expecting someone, but he thought I was going to be a man.'

'A man. . .?'

'Yes. . .Toni. . .'

'Oh, I see!' Hilary laughed. 'So he had a bit of a shock when you turned up.'

'He was quite rude, actually, because I am a woman. I got the impression he was fed up with women assistants—that they weren't in some way up to the job.'

'I hope you put him in his place,' replied Hilary indignantly.

'Too right I did—and I intend to show him that I mean it.'

'Good for you—that's what I like to hear!' Hilary stood up. 'Well, this won't do—I really came to see if you'd like to come for a walk before it gets dark. See a bit of Nairobi. We've been warned not to go out alone and certainly not after dark.'

'I'd love to, if you could give me half an hour to shower and change.'

'Sure. Oh, the other thing we've been warned about is not to wear any jewellery—especially gold.'

'OK,' Toni smiled, 'not that I have too much of that.'

'When we get back we have to meet Jack Christy in the bar so that he can give us details of tomorrow's travel arrangements.'

Toni hesitated, 'Did you say you were travelling down with us? Are you actually coming to Jabhati?'

'Yes, that's us our first port of call in Tanzania, then we are moving on to other bush stations to inspect sites where WaterAid have recently sunk boreholes.'

'Well, I must say it will be nice to have your company on the trip.'

The other girl left the room with a wave of her hand and Toni began to brighten up a little. This was her first visit to Africa, a place she had longed to see ever since she was a child, and she was determined she wasn't going to let Jack Christy's attitude spoil things for her. Hilary had thought him attractive and if she was really honest Toni had grudgingly to agree, but what she hadn't told the other girl was that she was right off men at the present time.

As she showered, Toni's thoughts inevitably turned to Martin Foster.

At one time she had thought her future mapped out: her career secure, marriage to Martin, possibly a couple of kids. Then it had all turned sour. Her relationship with Martin had ended—she had been heartbroken at the time; now she found herself doubting she had ever really loved him.

No, she thought as she lifted her face to the jet of cool water from the shower, men were definitely right off her agenda at the present time. And even if they weren't, Jack Christy would be the last person she would be interested in after the overbearing way he had treated her, and besides, hadn't Hilary said he and the exotic-looking Shakira were as good as married? In Toni's book that quite firmly put any man off limits.

Later they all met on the Jacaranda's bar terrace under a thatched roof and sat on cane chairs sipping long, cool drinks while they waited for Jack Christy.

Hilary Moss introduced Toni to the rest of her team—Paul Davis, a tall, thin, earnest-looking young man who viewed life from behind tiny, wire-framed spectacles, Henry Bowyer, a thick-set man of around sixty who already seemed to be having problems with the heat as he constantly mopped his face and neck with a large white handkerchief, and the ailing Ruth Galloway, a woman in her late fifties who from Hilary's description Toni felt she knew already.

To be sociable Toni asked if any of the group had been to Africa before.

They all shook their heads, then Hilary said she'd spent some time working in Cambodia and Henry irrelevantly mentioned that he had spent his honeymoon in Morocco some twenty-six years before.

'I can't say I'm happy about the food,' said Ruth, twisting in her chair to look over her shoulder into the hotel dining-room.

'Why? What's wrong with it?' asked Toni.

'Well, it's not what we expected, is it, Hilary?' Ruth glanced at Hilary Moss, who grinned unsympathetically back.

'Oh, I don't know, Ruth—it's exactly what I expected. The fish and chips last night was quite home from home I thought, but never mind, just wait till we get into the bush—the food there will probably be exactly what you were expecting!'

As Ruth shuddered and Toni bit back an impulse to ask Ruth why she had undertaken this trip, Paul Davis leaned forward, linked his hands between his knees and in his earnest fashion said, 'Do you happen to know how we are travelling tomorrow, Dr Nash?'

'Not really,' Toni replied slowly. 'I imagined by minibus—that seems to be the most usual form of transport from what we saw in Nairobi, doesn't it, Hilary?'

Hilary nodded. 'Yes, and we should see quite a bit of wildlife that way, Paul,' she said, then to Toni she added, 'Paul is a nature expert—he can't wait to see his first lion in its natural habitat.'

'Well, I hope the journey will be comfortable,' said

Ruth. 'The last time I travelled a long distance by bus was when I went to Scotland, and I ended up with a really bad back.'

'There won't be any fear of that tomorrow, Mrs Galloway.' The disembodied voice came from the foot of the veranda steps in the darkness of the hotel grounds. They all jumped and swung round in their seats and Jack Christy moved forward into the light and began to climb the steps to join them.

'Oh, Dr Christy!' Ruth gave a little shriek. 'I didn't know you were there.'

Paul Davis stood up and moved a chair forward, but as Jack Christy sat down his gaze fell briefly on Toni and she had the distinct impression that he had been standing in the darkness for some considerable time watching and listening to them all.

Henry Bowyer disappeared inside the hotel to order a drink for Dr Christy and as Toni glanced round she realised there was no sign of the woman, Shakira.

In incongruous contrast to Henry's open-necked shirt and Paul's T-shirt and shorts, Jack Christy was wearing tropical evening dress. The white of his suit accentuated his tan and his sun-bleached tawny hair; even his eyes, so bleak and grey earlier, now looked dark, the pupils wide in the half-light.

Instinctively Toni knew he would leave after this briefing, would leave to dine with the exotic Shakira who even now would be dressing for dinner.

A small movement beside her made Toni half turn and she was in time to see Hilary squirm in her chair as she gazed up in unashamed admiration at Jack Christy. Toni suppressed a smile.

'What did you mean, Dr Christy?' Ruth Galloway had leaned forward in her chair while fanning herself with a folded hotel menu. 'About there not being any fear of discomfort on our journey tomorrow?'

'Exactly what I said.' He flashed her a dazzling smile and as Ruth coyly lowered her gaze, Toni found herself wondering if his rudeness had been reserved exclusively for her. 'We won't be travelling by bus. . .' He paused as Henry returned from the bar. 'Thanks. . .' He nodded to Henry and watched by the others took a long draught of his drink.

'Eh, what's all this?' Henry sat down, looked from one to the other and mopping his forehead again, repeated, 'Not travelling by bus? How are we going to get there, then?'

'We've been offered a lift,' replied Jack Christy smoothly. 'A friend of mine runs a charter company—he has to go down to Harare in Zimbabwe to pick up some local dignitaries and bring them back to Nairobi for a conference. I have some medical supplies that I want taken down to Jabhati so he's agreed to take them and us.'

'That's jolly decent of him,' said Henry.

'Will it be comfortable?' asked Ruth Galloway suspiciously.

'Very comfortable, Mrs Galloway,' Jack Christy's reply was solemn. 'Lutas Charter Flights are the last word in luxury.'

The small-talk continued for about half an hour and, mellowed by her fruit cocktail, the perfumed fragrance of the flowering shrubs in the hotel grounds and the pleasant conversation of her newly found companions,

Toni felt herself relax. She was even beginning to wonder if she might have been mistaken about Jack Christy. He certainly seemed to have charmed Ruth Galloway and Hilary Moss. . .even the men seemed to be hanging on his every word. Maybe things were going to be all right after all. . .

Even as she was staring at him he suddenly rose to his feet and stood for a moment looking down at her. 'Could I have a word, please, Dr Nash?'

Startled, and only too aware of the silence from the others, Toni drained her glass, stood up then followed him from the veranda. They walked away from the hotel, past the swimming-pool and into the palm-fringed gardens, silent apart from the interminable singing of crickets and the distant hum of Nairobi's traffic.

As the soft darkness of the African night closed around them Toni felt her heart beating fast with apprehension. He'd been rude to her before—what his intentions were now she had no idea.

'Have you been to Africa before?' The question was curt, abrupt.

'No.'

'So why now? Why Africa?'

'I've always wanted to see Africa and I. . .I wanted a change from hospital routine——'

'If you're expecting this to be less demanding——'

'I'm not expecting anything of the sort,' she replied quickly, 'I'm quite prepared for it to be tough.' She paused, then suddenly, irritated by the hostility of his manner, she added, 'I know you don't want me here, know I'm not what you expected—but I can't help that. I am here, I gather there's a job for me to do and I intend doing it.'

'Oh, there's a job to do all right,' he said softly, 'make no mistake about that.' He fell silent then, and they walked on down a pathway softly illuminated by purple and blue lighting concealed in the shrubbery.

'What information did they give you about the bush station at Jabhati?' he asked at last breaking the silence.

'Not a great deal,' she admitted, 'only that it's south of Dodoma in the very heart of the Tanzanian bush, that people come from villages many miles away for treatment for themselves and their children—that water is scarce, food too, if their crops fail. . .'

'They didn't mention the flies,' he interrupted tersely, 'the heat, the lack of sanitation, the constant diarrhoea, the prejudice against white medicine? Shall I go on?'

'You don't need to,' she retorted. 'I can read, and I watch the television. I am well aware of the conditions you describe,' she added.

'Oh, so you know all about it,' his tone was heavy with sarcasm. 'That's good. . .we have nothing to worry about, then—there's no chance of a repeat performance of our last volunteer.'

Toni swallowed but remained silent, aware even in the darkness that he shot her a quizzical look.

'She couldn't stand the stomach upsets,' he went on at last.' She never did get used to the food, or maybe it was the water—that was before we had our borehole. . .then again, the volunteer we had after our borehole was sunk had to be transported back to London suffering from pancreatitis. . .and that was after her scare with the scorpion. . .'

'You needn't think you're going to put me off with these stories,' Toni replied icily. 'As I said, I have a job to do and I intend doing it.'

'Good. Just as long as you aren't under any illusions. Some women seem to have a false image of Africa—a romantic, glamorous image.'

'I'm not "some women", Dr Christy—I don't have any such illusions.'

He didn't answer, his very silence confirming that he remained unconvinced, while Toni found herself wondering just where the beautiful Shakira fitted into this scenario. Somehow she couldn't imagine her roughing it in some remote outpost, and she wondered briefly whether she had been one of the women with a false image of Africa whom Jack Christy had mentioned.

'I shall want to get away early in the morning,' he said abruptly, his tone implying a winding up of their conversation.

'Very well—that's no problem to me—I'm an early riser.'

'I hope the rest of the party are of a like mind,' he remarked, his tone implying that he doubted the fact.

'Hilary Moss said they were visiting Jabhati before travelling back to Dodoma.'

'That's correct—they are all representatives of various organisations interested in the work done by WaterAid and they are inspecting our borehole and noting the changes it has brought about to our way of life in the bush station.' His tone changed as he spoke of Jabhati, took on a note of pride.

'So did you travel up to Nairobi purely to meet them?' Suddenly she was curious.

'Why do you ask?'

'Well, I'm pretty sure it wasn't to act as my escort.'

'You're quite right,' he answered coolly as they turned and began walking back towards the lights of the hotel. 'I'm in Nairobi because I've been on leave up at Lake Victoria. The London office informed me that the WaterAid party would be here at this time and that you also would be arriving in Nairobi. It seemed sensible that we should all meet up and travel together.'

So that was why he was in Nairobi. She had wondered what had brought him there when she had been told to meet him.

As they climbed the veranda steps Toni suddenly had a mental picture of him holidaying with Shakira at some luxurious hotel at Lake Victoria and for some unknown reason she had to fight a sudden wave of irritation.

The terrace was empty. Jack Christy looked round. 'Looks as if the rest of your party have gone in to dinner,' he said. 'Would you like me to take you through?'

'That won't be necessary, thank you.' It came out more sharply than she had intended and he frowned. 'I'm sure you have other things to do—unless of course you intended dining with us.' As she spoke she allowed her gaze to flicker over his white evening suit.

'No,' he said evenly, ignoring the slightly mocking note in her voice. 'I have other plans.'

'I gathered as much,' she replied lightly. 'Goodnight, Dr Christy.'

He didn't reply immediately; instead, he seemed to be studying the blue cotton sundress she was wearing and as she turned, about to walk away, to her surprise he reached out his hand and with the back of his forefinger lightly brushed her thin shoulder-strap.

She froze, wondering what on earth he was doing, but before she had the chance to ask, he said, 'Don't wear this tomorrow.'

'I beg your pardon!' She stared at him, stung anew by his apparent effrontery and only too aware that his finger was now touching her bare flesh.

'I said don't wear this tomorrow.' He repeated it slowly, precisely as if he were talking to a child. 'You'll burn. Wear something sensible.'

Turning then and without a backward glance, he ran lightly down the steps and was swallowed up in the darkness.

Helplessly Toni watched him go, furious at his implication that she was anything other than sensible.

CHAPTER TWO

TONI spent a restless night and was awake, packed and ready to meet the others in the hotel foyer at the arranged time. Her talk with Jack Christy the previous evening had left her even more apprehensive about what she had taken on. It wasn't that she was having second thoughts about the posting; her apprehension came more from the prospect of working with the man himself rather than the nature of the job or its conditions.

They certainly hadn't got off on the right foot, she told herself ruefully; in fact Jack Christy had made it perfectly obvious that he didn't want her at the bush station and had then proceeded to do everything in his power to put her off.

But—she gritted her teeth—that was the last thing she would let happen. She would not only do the job and do it well, but in the process she would prove to Dr High and Mighty that she could do the job just as well as, if not better than, any man that the voluntary service cared to send.

'I really can't see why we need to travel so early.'

A discontented voice broke into her thoughts and when she looked round it came as no surprise to find Ruth Galloway struggling into the foyer with her luggage.

'I couldn't even find a porter—those boys are never

around when you want them—at this rate I shall hurt my back even before we start.'

'Here, Ruth, let me give you a hand. . .' Toni hurried forward and relieved the older woman of two of her bags.

With a sigh Ruth flopped down on to a sofa. 'As I was saying,' she glanced round the foyer, 'I can't see why we need to start out at this ungodly hour.'

'I expect Dr Christy is in a hurry to get back to the bush station,' replied Toni.

'Huh! You'd hardly have thought so just now,' snorted Ruth.

'What do you mean?' Toni frowned.

'He spent at least ten minutes outside canoodling with that fiancée of his. . .'

'Are you sure?'

'Quite sure.'

'Oh, well,' Toni shrugged, 'I suppose that's his business.'

'At least we won't have to put up with any more of it,' sniffed Ruth.

'Why?'

'He put her into a taxi.'

'A taxi?'

'Yes, a taxi. Do you have to repeat everything I say?'

'I'm sorry, I was surprised, that's all—I imagined his fiancée would be coming with us to the bush station.'

'I should say that's very unlikely after the lingering farewell I witnessed. Besides, could you see that spoilt creature dirtying her hands in some grubby outpost?'

'Well, no, I suppose not, but I assumed she would

want to be with him. . .' She trailed off uncertainly as Jack Christy himself suddenly appeared in the foyer. He stared at the two women as if he guessed they had been discussing him.

'Ah, Dr Christy.' Ruth seemed totally unperturbed. 'We were just saying how you must be wanting to get back to your flock.'

'My flock?' He frowned, and the two white lines between his eyes deepened into the tanned skin.

'Yes—on that bush station of yours.'

'Don't you mean my patients?'

'What? Oh, yes, I suppose so.' Ruth shrugged then glanced up as more people began arriving in the foyer. 'Here come the others,' she exclaimed.

Toni turned and to her relief saw Henry, Paul and Hilary making their way towards them. Something was needed to divert Ruth Galloway's tactlessness away from Jack Christy, who was quite obviously not in good humour after saying goodbye to his fiancée.

'So are we all here?' Jack Christy glanced round and as the doorman stepped into view and signalled to him, and a couple of porters apppeared to deal with their luggage, he said, 'The bus has arrived to take us to the airstrip.'

'Airstrip?' Henry Bowyer pushed his hat to the back of his head and frowned. 'Aren't we going to Nairobi Airport?'

'Not this time,' Jack Christy replied. 'Lutas Charter Flights operate from their own private airstrip.'

Ruth pulled a face and as they trooped out of the hotel Hilary giggled.

'I bet she won't like that,' she whispered behind her

hand to Toni. 'She'll expect a stewardess serving G and Ts complete with ice and lemon.'

A few minutes later Toni took her seat beside Hilary in the minibus and, glancing round to make sure Ruth wasn't in earshot, murmured, 'What I don't understand is how Ruth came to be on this trip in the first place. I wouldn't have thought this sort of thing would be her cup of tea at all.'

'Neither would I,' whispered Hilary, 'in normal circumstances, but it seems she wasn't to be outdone.'

'What do you mean?' Toni's eyes widened in amusement.

'Well, it appears she is the president of the ladies' branch of some international organisation that has been promoting WaterAid this year. It was tactfully suggested that it might have been more appropriate for the vice-chairman—who is fitter and ten years younger—to make this particular trip. . .but our Ruthie wasn't having any of that; she was determined to go come hell or high water.'

'I see.' Toni chuckled. 'Let's hope she doesn't live to regret it. I understand the beautiful Shakira has already opted out.'

'Shakira?' Hilary, rummaging in her rucksack, produced two cans of Coke, and as the bus drew away from the hotel offered one to Toni.

'Thanks.' Toni pulled the ring and waited for the froth to subside. 'Yes, according to Ruth, Jack Christy put her into a taxi at the crack of dawn after bidding her a fond farewell. For some reason I thought she would be coming to Jabhati with us.'

'Oh, I don't think that was ever the plan—I

understood they spent a short holiday at Lake Victoria, and now she's gone back to wherever it is she comes from, to do whatever it is she does—mind you——' Hilary took a mouthful of Coke and wiped the froth from her upper lip '—if Jack Christy were mine, I wouldn't let him out of my sight.'

'Maybe she doesn't like the idea of a remote bush station,' Toni remarked.

'Even so, if it were me, I'd follow him anywhere. . .' Hilary sighed, then gasped as the minbus lurched precariously round a corner, throwing the pair of them to one side and forcing everyone to hold on to the metal safety rails.

Even at that early hour Nairobi was a teeming mass of humanity as cars and taxis spewed fumes into the already polluted air amid a cacophony of sound. Dozens of minibuses like the one they were travelling in had taken to the roads, packed with eager tourists embarking on safari trips into the Kenyan bush.

'They don't look safe,' said Ruth as one overcrowded bus hurtled past them, its roof piled high with luggage and with grinning, shouting boys hanging from the sides. 'Makes me glad we're going by plane.'

'I just hope we'll still see plenty of wildlife,' shouted Paul above the sound of the engine.

'Don't worry about that,' called Jack Christy from his seat beside the driver. 'Even if you don't see much today, you'll make up for it during your stay.'

They had almost left the city behind when Jack Christy leaned forward in his seat and appeared to be giving directions to the driver.

Five minutes later, after driving through a maze of

unmade roads thick with the orangey-coloured dust that seemed to settle everywhere, they drew up outside a group of dark, shanty-style buildings. A group of youths lounging in the street and idly throwing stones at an empty beer can eyed them suspiciously.

With a muttered word that nobody understood, Jack Christy jumped down from the bus and disappeared inside one of the shacks.

He was gone for some time and one by one the group of youths sauntered over to the bus, tapping on the windows and trying to entice the occupants outside.

Their driver looked uneasy. 'You not go out,' he said apprehensively over his shoulder.

'No fear of that.' Henry wiped his face and this time Toni doubted it was from the heat.

She glanced round at the others and noticed that Ruth was wearing gold earrings.

Hilary followed her gaze. 'Trust her to think the rules don't apply to her,' she muttered.

By the time Jack Christy reappeared even Toni was feeling relieved, then as he climbed aboard she saw he was not alone.

'Hello,' murmured Hilary in her ear, 'who's he got this time? I must say Jack Christy's taste in women is flamboyant to say the least.'

She's hardly a woman, thought Toni as the young African girl followed him on to the bus. But she was beautiful. Quite beautiful, with her liquid eyes and smooth skin the colour of ebony. She was wearing an orange garment just visible beneath a voluminous blue cloak that was wrapped around her body, the front edge thrown over one thin shoulder. The sole extent of her luggage seemed to be tied up in a large bundle which she carried in one hand.

'This is Diaka,' said Jack Christy. 'She lives in Jabhati and she speaks no English. She will be travelling with us.' Something in the tone of his voice defied any argument and no one spoke.

He glanced round the bus, his gaze coming to rest on Toni, then he turned to the girl, gently touched her arm and said something in Swahili.

Toni recognised her own name, then he glanced at her again. 'She has not been well. I've told her you are a doctor and that you will look after her,' he said simply.

Toni nodded, suddenly ridiculously pleased that not only had he actually remembered she was there, but he had also acknowledged the fact she was a doctor.

Lutas Charter Flights occupied a site far to the west of Nairobi and consisted of a huddle of shanty-style buildings with corrugated iron roofs, which even at that early hour were shimmering in a haze of heat. Two aircraft were standing nearby, the sun glinting on their vast propellers.

'Good God!' Henry Bowyer stepped down from the bus and, tipping back his sunhat, scratched his balding head in disbelief. 'That's an old Dakota, isn't it?'

Jack Christy grinned. 'It is, and the other is a Caribou—wonderful, aren't they?'

'They look a bit rusty.' Ruth lifted her sunglasses for a better look. 'I sincerely hope they are safe.'

As she spoke a man came out of one of the ramshackle buildings. He must have heard what she said, for as he shambled across the tarmac strip to greet them he called, 'Safe as houses, ma'am, in fact a darn sight safer than some of these flimsy jobs they're using today. Good day, Jack, how are you?'

'Hello, Lutas, you old rogue,' Jack Christy clapped him on the shoulder, 'how's life treating you?'

The man grinned, implying that life was good. He was a bear of a man, not tall, but stocky and muscular. Telltale signs gave away the fact he was getting on in years; the dark tangle of hair that merged with his bushy beard was streaked with grey and his skin was lined, leathery. He wore a red and black checked shirt and bush trousers and Toni noticed that his huge hands were gnarled and ingrained with engine oil.

'Afraid there'll be a wait.' He looked round at the little group and as the minibus reversed and roared away in a cloud of dust Toni suddenly had the uncanny sensation of having been abandoned.

'How long?' Jack Christy frowned.

Lutas spread his large hands and shrugged. 'Electric storms,' he said, 'down near the border. No point taking off till they clear.'

'Can we wait inside, out of this heat?' asked Henry Bowyer anxiously.

'Sure.' Lutas jerked his thumb over his shoulder indicating one of the tin buildings behind him. 'Waiting-room in there—help yourself to refreshments.' He chuckled, then ambled off towards the aircraft, wiping his hands on an oily piece of rag.

The others watched him in silence then, just as Ruth Galloway opened her mouth to complain, Jack Christy turned towards the building and picked up his holdall. 'Right, come on,' he said firmly, 'let's get inside before we get eaten alive by these mosquitos.'

'Good idea.' Toni had spent the last few minutes slapping at the troublesome insects and she needed no second bidding.

It was a little cooler inside the building, an ancient fan suspended from the ceiling whirred noisily, but it was, as Lutas had implied, simply a waiting-room, with a bench that ran round the walls and a round cane table in the centre.

As they crowded inside, a tall African man rose from the bench and surveyed them through serious eyes.

Jack Christy nodded. '*Jambo.*'

'Good morning,' the man replied solemnly. 'My name is William Batouala.'

'Jack Christy.' They shook hands.

'I am travelling with you.' His English was clipped but perfect.

'To Jabhati?'

Toni noticed that Jack Christy looked surprised, as if he knew everyone at Jabhati and would have been informed of any newcomer.

William Batouala shook his head and briefly his gaze came to rest on Diaka who had silently followed them into the building and had sat down in the corner. 'No, not Jabhati—I come from Harare. I work for the government here in Nairobi, but my home is a village near Harare. I return because my mother is sick.'

'Well, I hope we're not going to have too long to wait,' said Ruth peevishly, looking round with obvious distaste at the sparsity of their surroundings. 'I don't suppose there's even chance of coffee in this Godforsaken hole.'

'Coffee through there. Lutas said to help yourself.'
William Batouala pointed to a doorway covered by a
beaded curtain in one corner of the building.

Toni looked at Hilary. 'Come on,' she said quickly.
'Let's go and see what we can find.'

They escaped to what turned out to be a tiny kitchen,
very basic, but with the necessary coffee-pot bubbling
on a stove and a shelf full of mugs.

'British Airways will have to watch out with compe-
tition like this.' Hilary chuckled and began to lift the
mugs down from the shelf.

Toni smiled and nodded. 'I think we could be in for
a very entertaining flight,' she remarked.

When they returned to the main room with two trays
full of mugs of coffee they found Jack Christy, Paul
and Henry helping to unload large packages from a
van that had just arrived outside.

'It's his medical supplies, apparently,' said Ruth by
way of explanation.

The coffee was surprisingly good and even Ruth
didn't complain, but afterwards came a long wait during which they had nothing to do but sit on the hard
benches, read, or talk.

Twice Toni attempted to communicate with Diaka,
but on each occasion, as she approached, the girl
merely lowered her eyes. The second time Toni tried
to suggest that in view of the heat Diaka might be
more comfortable if she were to remove her cloak, but
the girl's only response was to gather the folds of the
garment even more closely around her and in the end
Toni gave up. Jack Christy had said the girl had been
ill, but she gave no outward sign of any discomfort,

so Toni felt there was little she could do.

For a time they talked of their families or their jobs. They learnt that Henry had two daughters, one who had just got married, the other who was planning to marry early the following year.

'Expensive time,' Jack Christy observed, and Henry nodded.

'You can say that again—I've been working all hours to pay for it all.'

Ruth, not to be outdone, announced that all three of her children married within a year of each other.

'Do you have grandchildren, Ruth?' asked Toni.

'Yes, three, two girls in this country and a grandson who lives in Canada. I haven't seen him yet,' she added. 'I just don't seem to have had the time to make the trip. Ever since I became lady president life has become one mad whirl.'

Paul told them he was single and lived with his widowed mother.

They fell silent soon after that, and Toni realised that Jack Christy hadn't offered any information about himself.

It was early afternoon before Lutas appeared to tell them that he was preparing to take off. With sighs and groans they stretched and scrambled to their feet.

'Have the storms gone, Mr Lutas?' asked Ruth archly.

He gave a curt nod then solemnly said, 'Lutas, ma'am. Just Lutas.'

'I beg your pardon.' Ruth looked bewildered and as their pilot disappeared outside again it was left to Jack Christy to explain.

'That's what he likes to be called—just Lutas.'

'Why?' demanded Ruth.

'Wouldn't you if your first name was Cuthbert?' Jack Christy grinned.

It was the first time Toni had seen amusement on his face, and it transformed his features, giving a fascinating glimpse of another side to the rather grim, humourless man she had seen so far. Then it was gone, and he bent down to pick up his bags.

Diaka, who had not moved throughout the long wait, stood up and picked up her bundle, and the rest of them began sorting and collecting their own luggage.

As they were leaving the building Toni saw that Paul was searching furiously in his holdall.

'What's up, Paul?' she asked, noticing his worried expression.

'I've left my Ventolin inhaler at the hotel,' he replied without looking up.

'Are you sure?' She glanced down at the rest of his luggage.

He nodded miserably. 'Yes, I remember putting it on the windowsill in the bathroom, I must have forgotten to pick it up again.'

As they were speaking the others had all begun to walk across the tarmac to the waiting aircraft. Jack Christy, however, must have realised something was wrong for he came back.

'Is there a problem?' he asked.

'Paul's left his medication at the hotel,' Toni explained quickly.

'What medication?'

'Ventolin.'

'You're an asthmatic?' Jack Christy frowned.

Paul nodded, 'Yes, since I was a child.'

'Well, there's no time to return to the hotel.'

'Don't you have any Ventolin in those supplies?' asked Toni quickly, pointing through the open door towards the plane.

Jack Christy shook his head. 'No.'

Paul began to look increasingly anxious and Toni knew that anxiety could be the very thing to bring on the attack he was dreading. Before she could speak, however, Jack intervened.

'Don't worry, I have Ventolin at the station at Jabhati—we should be there in a few hours.'

'OK, thanks.' Paul's relief was obvious as they began to walk towards the aircraft. 'Luckily,' he said, 'I don't seem to have been affected since I landed in Africa.'

'Change in environment,' said Jack.

'Could be.' Paul gave a nervous laugh.

It was unbearably hot, the sun seeming to bounce off the tarmac as they hurried across to the plane. They were to travel in the Dakota and as Toni climbed aboard, the dimness and comparative cool of the interior seemed a welcome haven from the heat outside.

Henry seemed excited by the fact that they were flying in the Dakota and proceeded to explain in great detail to Ruth, who was sitting beside him, that his brother-in-law had many years before worked on the construction of Dakotas.

As Toni took her seat beside Hilary she heard Ruth reply that she was more relieved by the fact that Lutas had informed them that he had flown with the RAF in his younger days. In Ruth's book that made him fit to pilot the plane she was travelling in. Toni hoped Lutas hadn't heard her. It was doubtful he had above the noise of the engines and the shouts of his two African ground staff.

Moments later the aircraft bounced along the runway, gathered speed, lurched, bumped, then took off.

They soared into the white hot sky above Nairobi and Toni realised she was holding her breath.

Across the aisle, Jack Christy was sitting beside William Batouala, and as Toni breathed out she met his glance and knew he had been watching her. There was a faint frown on his face, as if he was again doubting her, doubting her strength, or her stamina to cope with what lay ahead. Ignoring his stare, she turned and casually looked out of the window, outwardly nonchalant, but inwardly seething and more determined than ever to prove him wrong.

CHAPTER THREE

WITHIN the first half-hour the coolness of the plane's interior had gone and the fierce heat of the afternoon sun turned the aircraft into an oven.

'God, it's hot!' Hilary took a mouthful of bottled water then sprinkled some on to a handkerchief and wiped it round her face and neck. 'We just take it for granted, don't we?' she grimaced as she replaced the top on the bottle and returned it to her rucksack.

Toni nodded in agreement. 'How long have you been with WaterAid?' she asked curiously.

'Nearly three years.'

'And what's your official capacity?'

'I'm an environmental health official.'

'I'm impressed.' Toni smiled. 'Now tell me what it means.'

'Well, this trip is purely an inspection one, but more often than not I travel to sites where we hope to sink boreholes. I talk to the inhabitants, decide with them where the borehole will be, then educate them in hygiene and make them aware of the benefits of clean water. You would be amazed at the differences it makes to their lives, apart from the obvious one of fewer tummy upsets.'

'Tell me about them.' Toni was interested, as she knew this aspect of things could affect her own work at Jabhati.

'For a start it can mean the women of a village have much more time on their hands.'

'How do you mean?' She threw Hilary a curious glance.

'It's always the women who fetch water.' Hilary warmed to her theme, her expression becoming animated. 'Sometimes they have to walk up to distances of ten kilometres to the nearest water-hole—as you can imagine, that takes a fair slice out of each day.'

'Yes, it would,' Toni agreed.

'Another difference is that after a borehole is sunk in a village the younger children and the toddlers are a lot cleaner—and the men!'

Toni raised her eyebrows. 'Tell me more.'

'Well, the women used to wash themselves at the waterholes when they collected their water; they would take their babies with them and the older children would go too. But in most cases it would be too far for the toddlers to walk, and the men wouldn't go to fetch water as that is considered women's work.' Hilary paused a moment, reflectively, then said, 'One of the saddest stories I heard was from an aid worker who came back from Africa and told of a woman who couldn't bear to kiss her little daughter because she was so dirty.'

Toni, humbled by the story, glanced across at Diaka, but the girl's expression remained impassive as she stared straight ahead.

Hilary too glanced round then stood up. 'I think I'd better go and talk to Ruth,' she muttered, 'she's look-ing a bit green round the gills. I'll go through our itinerary with her; that'll take her mind off the journey.'

As Hilary made her way down the aisle Toni leaned her head back and briefly closed her eyes. She could feel a trickle of sweat running down her neck while the cotton shirt she had chosen to wear, in the assumption that it would be cool, was already sticking to her breasts. She didn't, however, feel she could complain, especially after the story Hilary had just told her.

In spite of the heat in the aircraft she felt herself becoming drowsy and it was a light touch on her hand that brought her to. She opened her eyes and found Jack Christy leaning over her—his face only inches from her own. Startled, she gazed stupidly at him, noticing the clear grey of his eyes beneath the mane of tawny blond hair.

'What is it?' she asked in alarm. 'What's wrong?'

'Nothing's wrong,' he replied coolly. 'I simply thought you wouldn't want to miss the sights.' He inclined his head towards the window.

'Sights?' She turned her own head and looked down. The ground seemed alarmingly close and, as she attempted to focus, the whole landscape appeared to be one moving mass.

'What. . .?' She rubbed her eyes, suddenly aware of exclamations of excitement from other members of the group.

'Wildebeest. . .' breathed Jack Christy in her ear.

'Oh!' She watched in fascination as the herd moved *en masse* across the plain like some great moving sea.

'That's more like the Africa I expected,' she breathed at last.

'And you would have missed it.' There was a mocking note in his voice.

'I didn't imagine we would see anything like that from the air,' she retorted, defending the fact that she'd been asleep.

He gave a wry smile. 'Lutas is flying very low.'

'Is that permitted?'

'Of course not—it's totally illegal, but——' he gave a non-committal shrug '—Lutas is Lutas. He heard young Paul complaining he hadn't seen any wildlife yet,' he added after a moment, 'so he must have decided to make his day.' Even as he spoke the plane banked, circled, then veered sharply westwards.

'Oh, look, down there, giraffe!' Toni leaned sideways and excitedly clutched his arm. 'And there—isn't that zebra?' Amid cries from the others, she watched, enchanted, as Lutas circled once more, allowing them an even better view of the animals on the plain below; then, as the aircraft banked once again and began climbing, she sighed and leaned back. It was only then that she realised she was still clutching Jack Christy's arm, while he was watching her in amusement.

'I'm sorry,' she muttered, rapidly withdrawing her hand.

'Think nothing of it,' he replied smoothly. 'It's quite understandable that you should be excited—everyone's first experience of African wildlife is exciting.'

'And Jabhati?' She raised her eyebrows. 'Is that exciting as well?'

'It depends what you class as exciting,' he replied drily. 'We don't quite have the same wildlife of the plains and the grasslands, but then we are kept so busy we don't have a lot of time for watching animals.'

Something in his tone stung Toni into a swift response. 'I realise, Dr Christy, that I am going to Jabhati to work,' she said crisply.

'Good. You won't be disappointed, then: there's never a shortage of work.'

She threw him a glance. 'I've been talking to Hilary,' she said, 'about the differences that clean water supplies have made to the people in remote villages.'

'It's certainly made a difference in Jabhati,' he agreed.

'When did they sink the borehole there?'

'Only about six months ago,' he replied. 'It's still something of a novelty.' He glanced across the aisle as he spoke. 'Diaka will find life very different from what it used to be.'

Toni leaned forward to look at the girl. 'I've tried to talk to her,' she said slowly, 'but. . .' she shrugged, the gesture implying she hadn't got anywhere '. . .she seems happy enough; nothing seems to worry her.' She sank back into her seat.

'Believe it or not——' Jack Christy lowered his voice in spite of the fact that the African girl spoke no English '—she's terrified.'

'Terrified?' Toni looked sharply at him.

He nodded. 'She's never flown before—she's petrified.'

'Well, I'd never have known—she hasn't uttered a sound.'

'That's her way—there's a fierce pride with these people, as you will find out—if you stay, that is,' he added.

'What do you mean, if I stay?' she demanded angrily.

He shrugged. 'What I say. If you can stand the pace.'

'Dr Christy——' she took a deep breath '——I have every intention of standing the pace, as you put it, so I would be obliged if you would not bring the subject up again.'

He didn't answer immediately, instead standing up and looking down at her, but before moving away, irritatingly, he said, 'Time will tell.' Then, not giving her a chance to say more, he added, 'Oh, there is just one thing—if we are going to work together, you'd better drop this Dr Christy business—the name's Jack.'

He moved away then, back down the aisle to his seat beside William Batouala. Toni watched him go with a mixture of exasperation and renewed determination.

If anything the heat inside the aircraft intensified, and once again Toni found herself dozing. She was aware that Hilary came back to sit beside her but after that she was lulled by the hum of the engine.

The next thing she knew was the sound of Lutas's voice coming to them through a speaker over the door of the cockpit, telling them to look out of the window as they were flying near Mount Kilimanjaro.

'It's Africa's largest mountain,' he explained. 'Didn't think you'd want to miss it—it's pretty impressive.'

Toni craned her neck and through the window on the opposite side of the aisle, between the clouds, she was just able to see the snow-capped top of the mountain.

'We shall be crossing the border into Tanzania shortly but we'll be flying too high for you to see much—so I suggest you folks go back to sleep.' Lutas chuckled, a rich throaty sound that crackled through the speaker. 'I know that's what you were all doing. I'll wake you up when we get to Jabhati.'

The next thing she knew Hilary was nudging her. She opened her eyes. She had been dreaming that she was in her home town of Chichester, shopping with her mother. For a moment she couldn't think where she was. It was still unbearably hot. She half turned to Hilary. 'What. . .?' she began.

'Ssh. Listen.' Hilary nodded towards the cockpit and Toni realised that Lutas was talking to them again.

'Nothing to get alarmed about,' he was saying; 'those storms I was talking about earlier have decided to put in another appearance. Apparently there's a whole range of them at fifty-five thousand feet, which poses me a bit of a problem. I can't fly under them because there are a few mountains in the way, which means I have to make a detour. Afraid dinner in Jabhati could be spoiled tonight, my friends.'

There was no more sleeping after that. Hilary produced a bag of mint imperials from her rucksack, passed them round and everyone, with the exception of Diaka, took one.

'I don't like thunderstorms,' said Ruth. 'They always give me a headache. As a matter of fact I have a headache now. I'd put it down to the heat. . .'

'Wonder how far he'll have to detour,' mused Henry uneasily.

'Hope he's got plenty of fuel on board.' There was a trace of anxiety in Paul's tone.

They flew for about another hour without any further word from Lutas, and everyone had just come to the conclusion that all must be well when a huge flash of lightning lit up the interior of the plane and Ruth gave a loud shriek. It was only then that Toni realised just how dark it had become, great banks of purple cloud that seemed to envelop the plane. The lightning was followed by several loud claps of thunder.

'Looks as if these pesky storms are chasing us,' said Lutas through the speaker. 'Prepare yourselves for a rocky ride, my friends.' Even as he spoke, the aircraft lurched crazily and dropped in height.

Everyone began talking at once, then, as the plane bounced and was buffeted on all sides by the storm, one by one they fell silent.

They flew through the storm for about thirty minutes almost in total silence in the cabin.

Toni closed her eyes again and tried to relax, but it was impossible. When she opened her eyes she noticed the knuckles of Hilary's hands were white and strained as she clutched the strap of her rucksack. She looked round at the others, finding herself fearful of their reactions. Henry was sweating profusely, Ruth had her eyes closed and Paul looked ashen. William Batouala looked as if he might be praying. Only Diaka looked unaffected by what was happening.

Her gaze flickered back to Paul and she remembered the medication he'd left in Nairobi. As if at some hidden signal she turned and looked at Jack and as his gaze met hers she knew instinctively he was thinking the same thing.

He stood up and everyone looked at him. With his eyes he indicated for Toni to go to Paul, then in a casual voice, he said, 'I'll go and see how Lutas is doing,' before making his way to the front of the plane.

Toni stood up and squeezed past Hilary then moved across to Paul.

'Are you all right?' she asked quietly.

He nodded. 'Yes, I think so,' he replied, but he sounded shaky.

'Try and relax, Paul,' said Toni, hoping she sounded matter of fact. 'You'll be fine.' She knew that stress could bring on the asthma attack Paul was dreading.

Feeling helpless, she made her way back to her seat. It was a further ten minutes before Jack returned and when he did so they couldn't fail to notice how grim-faced he was.

'What's happening, Doc?' asked Henry Bowyer in an obvious attempt to sound jovial.

'The situation is serious.' Jack stood at the head of the aisle and faced them. 'Lutas was all for keeping it from you, but I feel it is your right to know what is happening.'

'What do you mean? What is happening!' It was Ruth who spoke, and there was no disguising the note of hysteria in her voice.

'For a start we are many miles off course,' Jack began.

'How many miles?' asked Henry.

'According to Lutas it could be hundreds of miles.'

'So where are we exactly?' Hilary shifted in her seat.

'He doesn't know,' replied Jack grimly.

There was a general chorus of dismay from everyone.

'What do you mean, he doesn't know!' Ruth's voice rose shrilly above the others. 'He must know—he's the pilot, for God's sake! You said he was a good pilot!' she finished accusingly as pandemonium broke out among the others.

'He is a good pilot!' Jack's voice cut through the noise and the others fell silent. 'He is a good pilot,' he repeated when he had their attention once more. 'No pilot could have done more than he is doing in the present circumstances.'

'So why doesn't he know where we are?' asked Henry quietly.

'Exactly. Why doesn't he know where we are?' demanded Ruth.

'He doesn't know where we are,' said Jack patiently, 'because some time during the storm we were struck by lightning and all radio contact was wiped out.'

Shocked silence greeted his statement. He glanced round, his gaze coming briefly to rest on Diaka who still hadn't moved.

'But. . .' it was Paul who spoke first only it didn't sound like Paul, the voice high, thin '. . .the compass. . .surely the compass. . .'

'The lightning damaged that too,' said Jack quietly, his gaze still on Diaka. 'The compass needle is spinning—it's meaningless.'

'So we're lost.' It was Henry who finally voiced everyone's fear.

'It would seem so,' replied Jack.

'Oh, my God!' A moan escaped Ruth's lips, threat-

ening to escalate into panic-stricken hysteria and as
the others began to respond, again Jack Christy com-
manded their attention.

'You are to remain calm,' he said. 'There is to be
no panic. Above everything, you will remain calm.'

'What is he going to do. . .Lutas?' Hilary's voice
was barely more than a croak, but everyone heard her
and waited for the answer.

As if on cue the speaker above Jack's head crackled
and spluttered and they all looked up.

'Well, my friends,' Lutas's voice filled the cabin.
'Jack will have put you in the picture and you'll all be
sitting there wondering what happens next. He will
have told you we are off course—hopelessly off
course—in fact, I have no idea where we are. The
options are twofold—we carry on flying until the fuel
runs out, or I attempt to land this old bus while we
still have daylight. That is what I have decided to
do. I will try to find a suitable landing place. My
friends. . .I want you to prepare yourselves for an
emergency landing.'

CHAPTER FOUR

THE speaker spluttered into silence while Lutas presumably began mustering all his resources for the onerous task ahead of him.

A tremor of fear rippled through the aircraft.

'We're all going to die.' It was Ruth, predictably, who voiced everyone's terror.

William Batouala began muttering to himself, no doubt praying in earnest now, and Paul began wheezing, his breath coming in short, sharp gasps. Diaka closed her eyes and Hilary half turned to Toni. Before she had the chance to say anything however, Jack stood up again and with a muttered exclamation disappeared into the cockpit once more.

Toni's mind was racing—jumbled thoughts that chased each other, round and round like tiny rodents trapped in a cage. Surely she wasn't going to die? She couldn't be going to die. She couldn't believe she had come all this way, had come to Africa to fulfil a dream, only to die in an aircrash deep in the bush.

Fearfully she peered out of the window, trying to fight the panic that was rising in her throat like bitter bile. The ground still looked a long way off—an endless brown landscape dotted with green clumps and what looked like jagged rocks, but which in all probability were hills or even mountains. If the plane hit one of those, surely it would explode. Dear God! She

47

closed her eyes and tried to pray but all she could think of was her mother, who was on holiday in Australia, and of how heartbroken she would be when they went to tell her that her only daughter had been killed. She wondered who would go. Would it be someone from the voluntary services or would it be the Australian police?

Sweat began to trickle between her breasts and she passed her tongue over her dry lips. And what of the others? Ruth, and the little grandson whom she'd never seen. . .Henry's daughter about to be married. . . Paul's mother. . .and Jack Christy. . .what of him? Who would tell Shakira? Would she be devastated to learn that her lover had been killed?

'I repeat, you must all stay calm.'

With a start she looked up and realised that Jack had returned from the cockpit and was talking to them again. He looked calm, but she noticed a pulse that throbbed furiously beside his jaw betraying his tension.

'Lutas is going to try to find a suitable spot to bring the plane down before he runs out of fuel.'

'He s-s-said an em-emergency l-landing,' stuttered Paul. 'Did he mean a c-crash l-landing?'

'There's nothing wrong with the plane,' said Jack firmly. 'Lutas is a very experienced pilot so there's no reason why he shouldn't manage a perfectly safe landing. Now, would you please all fasten your seatbelts, then when I give you the word I want you all to lean forward and protect your heads with your arms. . . like this. . .' He demonstrated the safety landing procedure.

'But we're lost. . .' wailed Ruth. 'He doesn't even

know where we are. . .who knows what's down there. . .?'

Instinctively everyone peered out of the windows.

'We'll worry about that when we get down,' said Jack briskly. 'First things first—top priority is a safe landing.'

Even as he spoke, the plane dipped and began to lose height.

Hilary clutched Toni's arm and there were gasps and cries of alarm from the others.

Jack disappeared back into the cockpit and Toni gritted her teeth and dared another look out of the window.

The ground was certainly much closer and as she stared she saw that some of the objects that she had thought were rocks were in fact moving and she realised they were animals. . .buffalo, she thought, and at one moment she even thought she saw elephants, but she was too petrified to even point it out to the others. Not that anyone would have cared. What had once been so important had now paled into insignificance in the fight for survival.

As the ground seemed to hurtle to meet them at terrifying speed she was vaguely aware of Jack at the top of the aisle again.

'Lucas is going to land!' he shouted. 'Brace yourselves!' Then he dived into a seat behind the cockpit.

Toni whimpered with fear, then leaned forward and lifted her arms over her head, aware that Hilary beside her was doing the same thing.

They hit the ground with a sickening thud, rose again, then lurched and skidded to the accompaniment of a high-pitched screaming noise until finally, to the sound of tearing metal and with bone-splintering impact, the plane shuddered to a halt.

There was nothing; nothing but silence.

Toni lifted her head and winced. Her body felt jarred, bruised. Was she alive or had she died? Was this silence heaven? Cautiously she turned her head. Hilary was still beside her, her arms over her head, her eyes tightly shut.

'Hilary?' she whispered fearfully, then to her relief the other girl opened her eyes. 'Are you all right?'

'I think so. I'm not sure.' Hilary gingerly began to move, then pulled a face.

Someone began moaning, a low-pitched, eerie sound, and Toni eased herself up out of her seat and looked round the interior of the plane.

There was slight movement from one or two of the others. Carefully she stretched, relieved to find she was in one piece although her shoulder ached and her back felt horribly jarred.

Hilary also seemed to be all right and William had eased himself out of his seat and was bending over Diaka.

Toni edged past Hilary and crawled into the gangway and saw that it was Ruth who was moaning.

'What is it, Ruth? Where are you hurt?' She pulled herself up on Ruth's seat.

'My neck. . .my neck. . .' the woman moaned again, and clutched the back of her neck.

'I want you to keep very still, Ruth,' said Toni. 'Do you hear me?'

At first Ruth didn't appear to have heard, then when Toni repeated the question she whispered, 'Yes.'

Toni knew there was a very real danger that Ruth could have damaged her spine and that she should be immobilised before she was moved. Jack would help her. Desperately she looked towards the front of the plane and saw Henry making his way towards her. He looked red-faced and appeared to be sweating profusely. 'I think Lutas is badly injured,' he said. 'There's a great hole torn in the side of the cockpit. . .'

'Where's Jack. . .?' Wildly Toni looked round. Paul was retching helplessly over the side of one of the seats and Diaka was deathly still, her eyes closed. . .but she couldn't see Jack Christy.

Frantically she leaned over the front seat where she thought he had been sitting, then to her horror she saw he was slumped half under the seat, wedged against the door of the plane.

'Oh, my God! Jack!' She crawled forward until she could see his face. For one dreadful moment she thought he was dead. Even his tan had paled, his eyes were closed and blood had oozed from beneath his hairline and was trickling down his face. Desperately she checked for breathing, then sought for a pulse at the side of his neck.

'Is he dead?' Hilary peered fearfully over her shoulder.

'No.' With a sigh of relief Toni found his pulse. 'No, he's been knocked unconscious.'

'Toni, we have to get out!' Henry shook her shoulder.

'What?' She stared up at him.

'These old Dakotas run on petrol—we could blow up at any moment!'

For one terrible moment her mind blanked and she stared helplessly up at him, then William's face appeared over Henry's shoulder and there was something calming about the expression in his eyes.

'I will get Lutas,' he said simply.

'But if he's badly injured. . .'

'We have to move him,' said Henry urgently. 'We have to get everyone out. I'll see to Dr Christy.'

Toni stood up as William disappeared into the cockpit and Henry knelt down beside Jack.

'Hilary,' she looked back down the aisle, 'you must help me with Ruth—I think she may have injured her neck—we have to keep her as still as possible. Paul,' she glanced anxiously in his direction and saw he had a white handkerchief pressed to his mouth, 'are you all right?' As Paul nodded her gaze flickered to Diaka and she saw to her relief that the African girl had got to her feet, was leaning forward, her arms around her body. Something about her posture struck a chord in Toni but she had no time for speculation. 'Will you help her, Paul?' she said urgently.

Paul, his face ashen, nodded again then they all moved. There was no panic as they each carried out their allotted tasks.

The door of the plane had become jammed but between them the men managed to force it open with the aid of a small axe hanging on a hook beside the door-frame.

With great difficulty Toni and Hilary immobilised Ruth as best they could, supporting her head with her own webbed belt, hurriedly pulled from the waistband of her skirt and secured beneath her chin.

Between them they carried her to the door then lifted her down to Paul and Henry who waited below.

Henry had already carried Jack Christy in a fireman's lift out of the plane then dragged him to the shelter of a belt of trees before returning for Ruth.

Carefully the two men carried the injured woman towards the same trees and set her down on the ground.

Toni, pausing just long enough to grab Jack's medical bag and her own rucksack, jumped from the plane and followed Hilary.

They ran across the open space of scrub but as they reached the comparative safety of the trees, Hilary turned and, shielding her eyes from the fierce sunlight, stared back towards the plane.

'Look!' she gasped. 'William has got Lutas out.'

Toni paused in her flight and saw the tall African standing in the doorway of the plane. He was carrying the pilot in his arms as if he was a baby, but even from that distance Toni could see that Lutas's trousers were torn and blood had seeped through the dark blue fabric.

A sudden shout went up from Henry. 'Hurry up, man! You'll be blown to smithereens!'

William hesitated for only a moment then, taking a deep breath, he set Lutas down, jumped from the plane, then dragged the injured man out behind him. As he began to pull the pilot across the scrubland, Henry and Paul ran back to help.

Toni watched with bated breath, any second

expecting the Dakota to explode in a ball of flames.

From her new vantage point she could clearly see the gaping hole in the front section of the plane torn by a group of jagged boulders when it had touched the ground, and one of its wings that appeared to have crumpled on impact. The plane had apparently then skidded along the scrubland before coming to rest in a large clump of bush and trees.

At that moment the men reached the shelter of the trees with Lucas, and Toni forgot the plane and turned her attentions to the injured pilot. The little that was visible of his face behind his beard and beneath the thick thatch of his hair appeared ashen. For a moment she wondered if he was dead, then as she crouched beside him she detected shallow breathing, then found a faint pulse.

'His legs are badly crushed,' she observed to Henry as he leaned over her shoulder. 'And it looks as if the control column has bruised his chest,' she added.

'I had trouble getting him out.' William had collapsed on the ground, his back against the trunk of a tree as he took great gasps of air.

Desperately Toni looked round. Her gaze flew to Jack Christy's still form.

If only he were conscious. . .then she looked at her fellow passengers. All of them were looking at her as if expecting her to take control.

She took a deep breath and sat back on her heels. Hadn't she wanted a chance to prove herself, though maybe not such a dramatic one!

Her gaze came to rest on Hilary, who as if sensing her predicament raised her eyebrows slightly.

'Hilary,' she said firmly, her tone betraying nothing of her inner turmoil, 'I would like you to stay with Ruth. Keep her as still as you can. Henry, help me here please with Lutas. I want to see the extent of his injuries. Paul——' she looked levelly at the young man '——I'd like you to go and sit quietly under the trees for a while.'

'But. . .I won't have any medication now. . .Dr Christy said he had Ventolin at Jabhati. . .'

'I shouldn't think for one moment you'll have an attack here,' she replied crisply, inwardly praying that she sounded convincing, hoping she could induce him to relax. 'You're not in cold, damp, polluted air now,' she added, smiling confidently, as he still looked far from convinced. 'You said yourself you hadn't been affected since landing in Africa. . .the hot air obviously suits you.' Briskly she turned to William. 'Do you know first aid?' she asked.

The African nodded.

'Good. I'd like you to go to Dr Christy and get him into the recovery position.'

Without a word they did as she asked them, accepting her professional lead without question.

With Henry's help she managed to remove enough of Lutas's clothing to enable her to see the extent of his injuries.

His left leg appeared to be badly crushed below the knee and was bleeding profusely, the splintered tibia clearly visible through the flesh. His right leg also had been injured but less severely with superficial lacerations.

'We must stop this bleeding—he's lost a lot of

blood already.' Toni glanced up at Henry.

'A tourniquet. . .?' he began, but she shook her head.

'No, a firm pressure pad. . .' wildly she looked round again, then she remembered the medical supplies aboard the plane.

Henry must have read her thoughts, for he shook his head. 'No, Toni, it isn't safe. . .you say a pressure pad? Would my shirt do?'

'It would be better than nothing, but. . .'

Before she finished speaking Henry was tearing off his shirt and folding it into a firm pad.

'Here. . .' He handed it to her and between them they managed to raise the man's legs by wedging several large stones under his feet. Then quickly Toni positioned the pad and applied it to the man's injured leg, staunching the flow of bright red blood that already was staining the earth beneath him.

'Toni!' A sudden shout from Hilary made her look up.

'What is it?' she called back, her voice echoing in the stillness.

'Ruth is in terrible pain—I don't think I can keep her still.'

'All right, Hilary,' she called. 'I'll be right over. Henry, you take over here. Firm pressure on the wound, that's right, like that.'

As Henry took over, she crawled across the grass and picked up Jack's medical bag from the ground where she had tossed it before examining Lutas. Quickly, she sprang the catches and peered inside.

'Thank God!' she breathed, noting that the contents included antiseptic solution, morphine, hypodermic syringes and needles. Scrambling to her feet, she began to hurry over to the spot where Hilary was kneeling beside Ruth. As she passed Jack Christy's form she saw that William had done as she had instructed and put the doctor into the recovery position. She would have to tend to him. . .but later. Now, Ruth had to be top priority.

Just before she fell to her knees beside Ruth she was vaguely aware of Diaka sitting beneath a tree with her back half turned to the rest of them. The African girl was very still, her profile set as she gazed out across the bush, and fleetingly Toni found herself wondering just what it would take to move her. Nothing so far seemed to have affected her.

The next moment she had forgotten Diaka as Ruth claimed her attention.

From her brief past experience of Ruth, Toni thought she would be complaining bitterly at her discomfort—that, she could have dealt with, but the woman was silent, white with shock and obviously in great pain.

Carefully, so as not to move Ruth too much, Toni examined her, then gave a sigh of relief.

'What is it?' asked Hilary anxiously.

'She's dislocated her shoulder,' replied Toni. 'I was really worried that she'd broken her neck.'

'What are you going to do?'

'For the moment, I'm going to give her an injection to ease the pain.' As Toni spoke she opened Jack's case again and took out the packet of disposable hypodermic needles, syringes and an ampoule of Papaveretum. 'Hilary, unbutton her skirt, please,' she instructed as she drew up the injection.

As Hilary began to unfasten the buttons the older woman opened her eyes and moaned.

'It's all right, Ruth,' Hilary reassured her as Toni took a cotton wool swab and soaked it in spirit from the bottle in Jack's case.

'I'm going to give you something for the pain, Ruth,' explained Toni, dabbing her thigh with the swab as the woman groaned again. 'Try and relax now. . .just a little scratch. . .there.'

Ruth cried out a few times then began moaning again, then gradually, as Toni and Hilary held her, her moans grew fainter and she slipped into oblivion.

'Well, at least I can control her pain for a while,' murmured Toni at last.

'What about Lutas?' Hilary glanced across to where Henry was still bending over the injured pilot.

'He's lost a lot of blood and there's no telling the full extent of his injuries.'

'Did you give him an injection?' Hilary's eyes flickered to the empty syringe on the ground.

Toni shook her head. 'Not yet. He's unconscious at the moment but he'll be in great pain when he comes round.'

'What about Jack?' Hilary tried to look over her shoulder.

'He's still unconscious as well. I must go and see to him now.' Toni gulped as the sheer helplessness of their situation finally hit her. 'Oh, God, Hilary, I wish I could get those medical supplies—I don't know quite what was there—but anything would help! We don't even have any water. . .'

'Here, wait a minute. . .take this. . .there's a bit left.' Hilary suddenly opened her rucksack and pulling out her plastic water bottle thrust it at Toni.

'Thanks. . .' Toni stood up and for a moment remained still, as for the first time she became fully aware of her surroundings.

The plane had come down in an area of thick bush interspersed by scrubland and belts of trees. Far behind the trees harbouring the Dakota, a sheer rockface, densely wooded, rose vertically into the sky.

Although it was late afternoon the sun still beat down relentlessly. Toni tipped her hat back and wiped the sweat from her forehead and as she did so her eye caught a movement high above in the white heat of the African sky. Shading her eyes from the blinding glare, she gazed upwards and saw four black shapes circling high above the rock face. She shuddered.

Hilary followed her gaze. 'Vultures,' she whispered hoarsely.

Toni nodded grimly, then, taking a deep breath, she said, 'They won't bother us, it's only dead bodies they scavenge and there won't be any of those here—not if I have anything to do with it.'

Purposefully she strode back to Henry and Lutas.

'How's the bleeding?' she asked.

Henry glanced up and she noticed the sun had caught the top of his scalp through the few strands of greying hair he'd combed across his head.

'I think it's easing up.' Cautiously Henry lifted one corner of the pad and peered underneath.

'Could you continue a while longer, Henry? I want to check on Jack.'

Henry nodded. 'Yes, OK. How's Ruth?' he added anxiously as Toni began to move away.

'She was in a lot of pain,' Toni paused, 'but I don't think it's as bad as I feared—I've given her an injection. She's dislocated her shoulder.'

'God, how awful!'

'Yes, but it's not so bad as a broken neck, which is what I thought she'd done at first. Henry, call me if Lutas starts to come round, won't you?' Once again she started to move away but again she paused. 'Where's your hat, Henry?'

'Eh?' He looked up, then as if he'd only just realised he didn't have his hat, he shrugged. 'I don't know. I guess I must have dropped it—it's probably in the plane.'

'Your head's burning. . .'

'Don't worry about that—that's the least of our worries,' he replied grimly.

'It could become a problem—I don't want you going down with sunstroke.' As she was speaking, Toni tore off the red and white neckerchief she was wearing and draped it over Henry's head.

He grunted in reply, Toni straightened up and with another anxious glance at Lutas, who was beginning to stir, she hurried across to Jack Christy and knelt beside him, turning him from the recovery position and propping his head and shoulders against the trunk of a tree.

His face still looked an unhealthy colour beneath his tan, and blood had trickled from a cut on his hairline down the side of his cheek, to the corner of his mouth and into the rough stubble that was forming across his jaw. Already flies were buzzing and clustering around the wound.

He groaned and his eyelids flickered and Toni realised he was beginning to come round. She felt a surge of relief.

Carefully she unscrewed the lid of Hilary's water bottle, then, realising she had nothing with which to wipe his face, she tugged her shirt from the waistband of her shorts and unfastened the two lower buttons. She then tipped up the water bottle, soaked one edge of the material and, leaning forward, slipped her hand behind his back, aware as she did so of the hardness of the muscles that rippled across his shoulders. Lifting her hand to the back of his neck, she gently began to sponge his face, wiping away the blood and at the same time investigating the wound on his forehead.

The cut wasn't quite as deep as she had at first feared and it looked clean. It had stopped bleeding and the blood had dried and congealed around its edges. Gently she pressed the skin, concentrating on the appearance of the cut, only too aware how quickly this sort of thing could become septic.

A slight movement to her left suddenly caught her eye and, transferring her gaze from the cut, she saw that Jack had opened his eyes and was staring at her face in a kind of puzzled wonder.

'Welcome back,' she said softly.

He frowned, blinked, then as if it were a great effort, tore his gaze from her face and glanced round. Then she felt his whole body stiffen.

'What happened?' His voice was hoarse, ragged.

Still leaning over him, one hand supporting his head, she attempted to explain. 'Lutus crash-landed the plane—he's been injured—you were knocked out.'

'The others. . .?' Alarm flickered in his grey eyes.

'Ruth has dislocated her shoulder. . .I found morphine in your bag and gave her a shot. The others—well, shock mainly, nothing else too serious. . .except for poor old Lutas, of course. . .his legs are badly smashed up. I didn't have anything else. . .we had to get out of the plane in case it blows up. . .'

He stared at her as if he was having difficulty taking in what she was saying. 'You mean everything is still in the plane?' he said at last.

'Except for some hand luggage and your medical bag—I did manage to grab that at the last minute.'

She thought he would be pleased at her quick thinking. Instead, he struggled to get up, then when the effort was too much he sank back against the tree and stared at her.

'What's the matter?'

'You're saying everything is in the plane including the emergency survival kit and the water container?'

'Well, yes, I suppose it must be.'

'So what's that you've got there?' His gaze flickered to the plastic container in her hand.

'Oh, this is Hilary's water bottle.' She glanced down and suddenly became aware that, where she had pulled her shirt up to use as a sponge, she was revealing her bare midriff and most of her bra and that Jack Christy was staring at her with an incredulous expression on his face. Hastily she pulled her shirt back into place.

'So that's all the water we have?' he said at last.

'Yes. . .' She nodded. 'I suppose it is. . .'

'Then what the hell are you doing wasting it?' he demanded angrily.

CHAPTER FIVE

'WHAT do you mean?' indignantly she stared at him. 'I'm not wasting it—in case you're unaware of the fact, you have a cut on your head. I was simply cleaning it.'

'Save it,' he replied tersely.

'But a cut could easily turn septic. . .'

'I said save it.'

'There's only a drop left anyway.' She held up the container for him to see. 'It's hardly worth making a fuss about.'

'Every drop of water is precious in this country— make no mistake about that.'

'I know that, but I considered I was using it wisely.'

Stung by his attitude, which to Toni appeared most ungrateful, she sat back on her heels and watched as slowly he climbed to his feet.

'I'll remind you of that when you're gasping for something to simply moisten your lips, let alone to drink.' He stood for a moment looking down at her, swaying slightly as he tried to regain his balance.

She frowned up at him, then, shielding her eyes from the sun, she said, 'Surely it won't come to that.'

He shrugged, then winced as if even that simple gesture jarred his head and caused him pain. 'Who knows? Life and conditions in this country are totally unpredictable—for us humans anyway. It's different for the animals; they know what to expect. . .' He narrowed his eyes and stared around him, for the first time taking in his surroundings, his gaze travelling from the other passengers beneath the shelter of the flat-topped thorn trees to the damaged Dakota.

'Where's Diaka?' he said at last.

'Over there.' Toni pointed to the tree where the African girl sat and had to fight a sudden totally unreasonable surge of irritation that Jack's first concern should be for her, when she of all the passengers had done the least to help and still seemed completely unconcerned about the fate of anyone else.

'Is she all right?'

'She seems to be,' she replied shortly, then, not giving him the chance to say more, went on, 'Really it's Lutas I'm concerned about, and Ruth of course. . .'

But Jack didn't seem to be listening to her. Instead, he had lifted his face to the slight breeze that stirred the dust and appeared to be straining to hear some far-off sound. When she would have continued talking he held up his hand to silence her.

'What is it?' she whispered after a while. 'What are you listening for?'

'Lion,' he replied.

'Lion!' Her eyes widened. 'Here?'

'Of course.' He raised one eyebrow. 'What did you expect? We are in the heart of the African bush. Lion were here first.'

'Yes, I know,' she mumbled, suddenly feeling very foolish.

'I need to talk to Lutas,' Jack muttered, as much to himself as to her.

'I don't think he's come round yet.' She scrambled

to her feet and, glancing warily around, afraid now
that a lion might suddenly pounce from behind one of
the thorn bushes, followed him across the expanse of
scrub to where Henry was still kneeling beside Lutas.
Until he'd mentioned it, she hadn't given a thought to
the presence of animals, which, now she considered
it, had been ridiculous, for, as Jack had just pointed
out, they were in the heart of the bush.

They reached Henry and Lutas, however, without
mishap and as Henry looked up Toni saw the unmistakable look of relief in his eyes when he saw that Jack
Christy had regained consciousness.

'You OK, Doc?' Henry was apparently oblivious
to the incongruous picture he presented with Toni's
neckerchief draped over his head.

'Yes, thanks.' Jack crouched beside Lutas who
appeared now to be semi-conscious.

'I don't know if the bleeding has stopped. . .' Henry
tried to ease himself into a more comfortable position.

'Let's have a look.' Jack took over the pressure pad
and lifted it gently. 'Yes,' he confirmed after a
moment, 'it's easing up. Hello, old man,' he added as
Lutas opened his eyes.

Toni, watching, noticed the pilot's grey-tinged pallor, but at that moment a shadow fell across them
blotting out the sun. They all looked up and found the
tall form of William Batouala towering above them,
his face a serious mask.

'Dr Christy. . .?'

'What is it, William?' Jack frowned.

'It will soon be nightfall.'

'Yes, William, I know.'

'We must think of shelter.'

'Do you have any suggestions?' Jack stood up and faced the tall African, but it was a voice from the ground that answered his question.

'Plane the best shelter.'

It was Lutas who had spoken. It had obviously required a great effort and they all looked down at him. He had closed his eyes again and his body was rigid with pain.

'But we can't.' It was Henry who replied. 'The plane might blow up.'

Lutas gave a great sigh. 'Once the engine's cooled. . .won't blow up. . .couple of hours or so. . . Check tank for leakage. . .then get back inside. . . safest place. . .'

'Thanks, Lutas, old man,' said Jack gently, 'that's what we'll do.'

'You mean we got everyone out here for nothing?' Henry exploded.

Wearily Lutas shook his head. 'Could have gone up. . .sky-high. . .' he lifted his arms to demonstrate, but the sudden movement made him bellow with pain.

'Give me my bag.' Jack turned to Toni, who picked up his bag and passed it to him.

'Let's give you something for the pain.' Swiftly Jack opened the bag and took out a syringe and a morphine ampoule as Toni had done for Ruth.

While he was drawing up the injection, however, he kept talking. 'Lutas, before we knock you out, can you give us any idea at all where we are?'

Lutas, gasping, shook his head. 'Not sure. . .hundreds of miles off course. . .north-west Tanzania somewhere. . .maybe tip of Serengeti. . .don't know. . .sorry, my friends. . .'

'It's all right, old man. . .you did your best and thinks to you we're all alive.' As he spoke, Jack administered the injection into Lutas's thigh. 'Get some rest now; later we'll see about some splints for those legs.'

As Lutas sank into blessed oblivion, Jack began further examining the man's injuries, then as William touched his arm he looked up.

'What is it?'

'Diaka—you come.' William pointed.

'Right.' Jack stood up.

'I'd like you to look at Ruth as well,' said Toni quickly.

'Can't you deal with her?' Coolly Jack met her gaze and it was Henry who, glancing from one to the other, intervened on Toni's behalf.

'Toni's been absolutely brilliant, Jack,' he said. 'She organised everything. Without her, I reckon poor old Lutas here would have bled to death.'

'It's no more than I would have expected,' replied Jack evenly. 'Toni is a doctor.'

'Yes, I know,' blustered Henry, 'but she's only human and she'd been through the crash the same as the rest of us—I thought she was bloody marvellous.'

'Yes, quite,' Jack's tone softened slightly and Toni found herself wishing that Henry would shut up. She didn't need him singing her praises especially to Jack Christy.

'Now, if you don't mind, I must go and see Diaka,' said Jack, pulling his hat further forward. 'Henry, you stay with Lutas to watch for more bleeding. William,

you go and check the Dakota's fuel tank. Take young
Paul with you; it'll give him something to do and take
his mind off his asthma.' He glanced over to where
Paul was sitting on the ground with his head in his
hands. 'Toni, you go to Ruth,' he added. 'I'll join you
in a moment.'

He walked away with his long, easy stride, apparently now recovered from his concussion.
Automatically he'd taken control, and Toni found she
was relieved to have him do so. For a while her own
adrenalin had taken over and she had acted mechan-
ically without a thought for herself. Now, as she stood
up and began to make her way back to Ruth and
Hilary, she was dismayed to find she was trembling.

'What's happening?' Hilary's round face, glistening
with sweat, was anxious as she peered up at her.

'We've all got to get back into the plane,' said Toni.
'Apparently it's safe once the engine's cooled down,'
she explained as she saw Hilary's surprised expression.
'The men are checking for fuel leaks.' She glanced
down. 'How's Ruth?'

'Out for the count.' Hilary grinned. 'I don't know
what was in that shot you gave her but it sure knocked
her out.'

'It's a good job it has. I'm hoping we'll be able to
put her shoulder back while she's sedated.' She paused.
'Are you all right, Hilary?' she added.

'Me? Yes, fine, never felt better, apart from these
damn flies, that is.' Angrily Hilary flapped at the large,
reddish brown flies that swarmed around herself and
Ruth, then added, 'Quite an adventure, this—isn't it?'

'Hmm, one that most of us could have probably

done without,' replied Toni wryly.

'So what do you think is going to happen?' Hilary asked suddenly.

Toni looked up sharply and saw that Hilary's grin had disappeared and she looked anxious.

'What do you mean?' Toni hesitated, playing for time.

'Well, to us—now. I presume the aircraft can't be flown again.'

Instinctively they both turned and looked towards the Dakota that was just visible, a gleam of silver through the trees.

'That wing looks pretty buckled,' Hilary went on, 'and besides, even if it could be flown again, I shouldn't think poor old Lutas could oblige.' She paused. 'Could he?' she added hopefully.

Toni shook her head. 'No, he couldn't,' she said quietly. 'You're quite right, Lutus is badly injured.'

'Seems as if Jack Christy is OK now.' Hilary craned her neck to look at Jack who was crouching beside Diaka. 'That's one blessing.'

'Yes,' Toni agreed, 'he's all right. I should imagine it would take more than a bang on the head to put him out of action.'

'Do you think he can pilot a plane?'

'Probably.' Toni pulled a face. 'He sees to be able to do everything else.'

'You don't sound very keen on him.' Hilary raised her eyebrows.

'It's not that. . .' Toni shook her head in irritation. 'It's just that I can't seem to do anything right where he's concerned.'

'How d'you mean?'

Toni hesitated, uncertain for the moment just how much she should talk about her new boss, then, remembering how disappointed and even hurt she'd been by his attitude, she launched in.

'Well, first I almost found myself apologising because I was a woman and he wanted a male assistant, then when I got enthusiastic about being in Africa he informed me I was here to work, then to crown it all, just now, I was trying to clean the cut on his head with a drop of the water you gave me and he moaned at me for wasting water—honestly, Hilary,' she sighed, 'I just can't win where he's concerned.'

'Was he really worried about the water situation?' Hilary frowned.

'Apparently so. He said every drop was precious in this country.'

'Well, he's right there. . .but. . .' she trailed off, the sentence unfinished.

'But what?' Toni frowned and threw the other girl a sharp glance. 'What's wrong, Hilary?'

'It just makes me wonder how long he thinks we'll be here. . .' Hilary bit her lip and instinctively they both found themselves glancing up at the black shapes that still circled high above the rock face behind them.

'Oh, come on!' Toni exploded at last. 'We mustn't start thinking like that, we must be positive. I expect the radio will be working again now and we'll be able to radio for assistance,' she added cheerfully.

'Jack's coming over now,' said Hilary as Jack Christy began walking towards them.

When he reached them he nodded at Hilary.

'Are you OK?' he asked briefly, and when she nodded in reply, he crouched beside Ruth, took her pulse, ran his hands expertly over her neck and shoulders then glanced up at Toni. 'You're quite right,' he said, 'she's dislocated her right shoulder. This could be a good time to put it back,'

'Yes, I thought the same thing,' Toni agreed.

'Would you like me to assist?'

She stared at him in surprise; she hadn't for one moment imagined he would allow her to do it. 'You mean for me to do it?' she asked, aware of Hilary's amused glance.

'Why not? That is if you feel able to.'

'Of course,' she muttered. 'I have done it before.'

'Right. I'll pull, you manipulate.' As he spoke Jack moved behind Ruth and took hold of her right arm, easing it into the correct position.

As he did so Ruth stirred and opened her eyes, and Toni knew they would have to be quick.

She kneeled down by the injured woman's side then, taking a deep breath, she took hold of her shoulder, gently probed until she found the joint, then located the socket. She glanced up and her eyes met Jack's.

'Right?' he asked, and when she nodded, he braced himself. 'Now!'

The click as the joint went back was clearly audible, while Ruth, jerked fully now out of her state of sedation, gave a sharp cry of pain.

'It's all right, Ruthie,' said Jack gently, smoothing back the woman's hair as if she were a small child. 'You'll be OK now. We'll get some strapping out of the medical supplies in a moment to make you more comfortable.'

'Oh, my God,' moaned Ruth, 'what in the world happened to me?'

'You dislocated your shoulder,' explained Jack. 'Dr Nash has just put it back for you.' He glanced up as Paul suddenly appeared at their side. 'What is it, Paul?' he asked.

Paul hesitated and glanced nervously at Ruth, clearly uncertain as to what had just happened.

'William said to tell you,' he began at last, his eye still on Ruth, 'that the fuel tank on the plane is intact and there hasn't been any leakage.'

'Good.' Jack carefully moved Ruth into a more comfortable position, then he stood up and looked up at the sky. 'I'd say we have about two hours before it gets dark; Paul, I want you and William to find something for splints for Lutas.'

As Jack and Paul moved away, Hilary turned to Toni and grinned. 'Looks as if you finally got something right,' she said.

'What do you mean?' Toni frowned.

'You were saying you couldn't seem to do anything right as far as Jack Christy was concerned. . .but you don't seem to have done too badly with Ruth's shoulder.'

'It's all part of the training.' Toni shrugged.

'Well, I'm impressed.' Hilary drew her lips into a firm line and nodded. 'And I think Jack was as well,' she added.

'Oh, don't you believe it.' Toni gave a short laugh. 'It won't have meant a thing to him. He would have expected me to know how to do it.'

'Had you really done one before?' asked Hilary
curiously.

'As it happens, luckily, yes, I had, and quite recently
too, during a spell on Casualty. I dread to think what
he would have said if I'd had to admit I hadn't done
one.' Toni gave a little shudder. 'He would never have
let me forget it.'

There was no time for any further speculation then
as Jack allocated tasks and they all unquestioningly
obeyed his commands.

Toni re-entered the aircraft and after Jack had
broken open the wooden packing cases she unpacked
the medical supplies. She found the supplies mainly
consisted of dressings, syringes and other surgical
appliances but very little in the way of medication. She
found a triangular bandage which she took outside and
applied to Ruth's shoulder.

'This should give some support,' she said as she
fastened the safety pin.

'Is that right that we have to get back into the plane?'
asked Ruth peevishly.

'Yes, it's the safest place, according to Lutas,'
replied Toni.

'I wish they'd make up their minds,' grumbled
Ruth.

'Don't get up, I'll get two of the men to lift
you back into the plane.' Toni stood up then as
Hilary walked towards them, she looked beyond her
to where Jack, Paul and William were working over
Lutas.

'What's going on over there?' she asked Hilary.

'A bit of improvisation. William and Paul have dismantled two of the seats from the aircraft and Jack is going to use the metal uprights as splints for Lutas.'

During the next hour the men carried first Lutas then Ruth back to the plane.

As Ruth was gently lowered into one of the seats of the Dakota she caught at Toni's hand. 'Could I have a drink?' she gasped.

Toni glanced at Jack and he nodded. Quickly she unscrewed the top of Hilary's water bottle then holding it to Ruth's lips she carefully tilted it while the woman drank thirstily.

The others watched then as Ruth finished drinking and leaned her head back Jack said, 'I think this might be a good time to talk about rationing.'

'Rationing?' Paul looked up sharply. 'How long are we going to be here, for God's sake?'

'We don't know, Paul,' said Jack quietly, 'that's the whole point.'

'But surely it won't be too long?' There was a note of desperation in Paul's voice. 'Henry is trying to sort out the radio now—once we radio in, it'll only be a matter of time before someone comes for us.'

'Won't someone be looking for us now?' asked Hilary. 'Surely when we didn't land at Jabhati the authorities would have been alerted?'

'I'm sure you're absolutely right,' replied Jack calmly. 'I'm pretty certain they will have started a search—the problem is, they don't know where we are, and even if we can get the radio working, we could still have a problem, because we don't know our exact position. What is certain at the moment is that we will be here tonight, at least, so we need to organise ourselves.' He glanced round at the silent group. 'The first and most important thing in a situation like this,' he went on when nobody spoke, 'is shelter, and thankfully we have that.' He looked up at the ceiling of the plane. 'This should protect us from adverse weather conditions and any unwelcome attention from the local wildlife.'

'Oh, my God. . .' moaned Ruth faintly.

'The next thing is establishing our location. Henry, would you have a look at the radio? I believe you said you have some experience in that field.'

Henry nodded. He had removed Toni's neckerchief on entering the plane but he still looked hot and his skin was red.

'I'll see what I can do,' he said.

'The third thing,' Jack went on, 'is water, and the fourth is food. Now——' he glanced at the ring of silent faces again '—as I'm sure you are all aware, we can survive for some considerable time without food, but we can't last for long without water.'

'There's the emergency container. . .' began Paul optimistically, and everyone turned and looked at the plastic drum at the rear of the cabin.

'Exactly,' replied Jack. 'In that, we have the equivalent of roughly a litre of water per person.'

'Thank goodness for that,' said Paul with relief.

'But it still has to be rationed,' replied Jack, 'because we don't know yet just how long it will have to last.'

'It won't be that long, for God's sake!' Ruth's voice from her seat was barely more than a hoarse whisper.

'When my husband knows I'm missing, he will organise the biggest search ever.'

'And he might not,' muttered Paul, then fell silent as Hilary giggled hysterically and Toni shook her head at him.

'As far as I know,' Jack went on when he had everyone's attention again, 'we don't have very much food on board. What I would like you to do now is to go through your luggage so we can pool our resources—I want every packet of sweets, every biscuit, every bag of crisps you can find. Oh, and I want everyone to try and find a drinking container. Toni, perhaps you and Hilary can organise the food and water.'

Toni nodded and scrambled to her feet but Jack hadn't finished and he held up his hand. 'Another thing you need to do is cover up. Some of you are only wearing shorts and T-shirts—I suggest you all wear trousers and long-sleeved garments—by rights, there shouldn't be so many mosquitos in Tanzania as there are in Nairobi, but you can't be too careful. It will also get much colder after nightfall so look out a warm jersey from your luggage.' He looked round, his eye coming to rest on William.

The African had been sitting on the floor of the plane, his knees drawn up to his chest, his head resting on his hands while listening to Jack, and now he raised his head.

'William, would you show Paul how to dig a latrine? Use the axe to break up the surface soil then dismantle one of the medical supply crates so that you can use the wood as spades. Build it well behind the aircraft.' Jack paused and glanced round again. 'And while we're on the subject, none of you women will go there unaccompanied—is that clear?'

Toni and Hilary nodded, but Ruth's shudder was probably more at the thought of the primitiveness of the latrine than of the possible dangers of the bush. 'What about washing?' she asked faintly.

'There will be no washing.' The firmness of Jack's tone belied any argument. 'Now, let's get cracking,' he added, 'before it gets dark.'

Paul stood up, then glanced sharply around, the last of the afternoon sunshine glinting on his glasses. 'Where's Diaka?' he asked as if he had suddenly just realised the African girl wasn't in the plane.

'She's all right,' said Jack quickly. 'She's still sitting outside.'

'But shouldn't she be listening to this?' sniffed Ruth. 'I presume it all applies to her as well.'

'She doesn't understand any English,' began Hilary doubtfully, 'but I must admit, I do think she should at least be attempting to pull her weight, the same as the rest of us.'

Toni threw Jack a quick glance and saw his mouth tighten.

'Jack,' she began hesitantly, some instinct warning her of his reluctance to talk about the African girl, 'you said when Diaka first joined us that she wasn't well. Can you tell us more?'

They all waited, curious now, aware that some mystery surrounded the girl.

Jack was silent for a moment, then, as if reaching a sudden decision, he took a deep breath. 'Maybe I misled you when I said Diaka was unwell,' he said, 'because that isn't strictly true. But the reason she hasn't been pulling her weight, as you put it, is because she is eight and a half months pregnant.'

CHAPTER SIX

OF COURSE! She should have known. Would have recognised it if only she had given herself time to consider the facts; the voluminous cloak drawn around the thin body, the reluctance to part with that cloak in spite of the heat and the way, after the crash, Diaka had clutched her stomach, not in pain but to protect her unborn child.

In the stunned silence in the cabin of the Dakota everyone, with the exception of William, gazed at Jack Christy in astonishment. William simply nodded. In the end it was Henry who broke the silence.

'But she's barely more than a child herself! Why didn't you say?'

'Lutas wouldn't have taken her if I had,' Jack replied simply. 'She poses too much of a risk.'

'You can say that again,' said Hilary.

'How is she now, Jack?' Toni frowned as the full implication hit her.

He shrugged. 'How you would expect. She's in shock that's why I've tried to keep her quiet.'

'This is all we need!' cried Ruth. 'If she decides to give birth we'll need gallons of hot water.'

'I think you'll find that assumption is grossly over-exaggerated,' replied Jack drily. 'But certainly Diaka will need all our support,' he glanced at Toni. 'How's your obstetrics, Dr Nash?'

'Pretty good, actually,' she replied. 'My last post was in Maternity.'

'Good,' he said crisply. 'In that case, would you go and see Diaka and try and make her understand that you will help her?'

As they all began to carry out Jack's instructions, Toni left the plane and walked across the scrubland to the longer grass beneath the thorn trees where the African girl was still sitting staring into the bush.

The great orange orb of the sun was setting rapidly, falling beneath the far horizon, and the girl's profile against the crimson flush of the sky looked as if was carved from ebony. There was not so much as the flicker of an eyelid as Toni crouched beside her.

'Hello, Diaka,' she said softly, at the same time lifting the girl's hand and holding it between her own. Still there was no response, then with her other hand Toni gently touched the front of Diaka's cloak. Immediately she felt the size of the mound beneath.

The girl then turned her head and looked at her.

There was unmistakable fear in the liquid, dark eyes as she realised that her secret was out.

'It's all right, Diaka,' said Toni softly. 'I will help you, and your baby.'

Diaka might not have been able to understand Toni's actual words but there must have been something infinitely comforting and reassuring in her tone. The flicker of fear died in the girl's eyes and when Toni tightened her grip on her hand she allowed her to help her to her feet. On the short walk from the thorn trees to the aircraft Toni talked continuously, quietly, one arm around Diaka, supporting her.

As they approached the aircraft Toni saw that Jack was building a pile of wood on the scrubland and guessed he was about to light a fire. William and Paul appeared through the trees from the rear of the plane, large pieces of packing case in their hands which they tossed on to the pile.

Without a word the men helped Diaka into the plane where Hilary was waiting with water for the girl to drink in the plastic top from a bottle of mouthwash that Ruth had found in her luggage.

'I think everyone has a container for drinking now,' said Hilary. 'Some are more salubrious than others,' she grinned as she handed Paul an empty Coke can, 'but at least we all have something. I'll use this to measure the water so that everyone has the same.' She held up the plastic top from her own water bottle. 'Jack and I reckon it holds about five fluid ounces. Your containers will be filled twice a day.'

'It's up to you when you drink it,' said Jack, suddenly appearing in the doorway of the plane, 'but I strongly advise you to make it last—only take a drop at a time, don't guzzle it all at once.'

'What food have we got?' asked Toni.

'Not very much.' Hilary pulled a face. 'So far only sweets, three packets of crisps, two apples and a black banana.'

'Have you looked in the cockpit?' asked Jack.

'No.' Hilary shook her head. 'Do you think Lutas might have had something?'

'Probably.' Jack glanced down at Lutas but he was still asleep. 'Let's have a look.' He turned away but before he could enter the cockpit Henry appeared, blocking his path.

'Any luck with the radio?' asked Jack and everyone paused, waiting for Henry's reply.

He shook his head and a ripple of disappointment ran round the cabin. 'No, nothing, I'm afraid,' he said, 'it's absolutely dead. I think it must have been damaged in the landing.'

'Never mind,' said Jack briskly. 'Try again later. Did you happen to see any supplies in the cockpit?'

'There's a box in there,' Henry replied. 'I'll have a look.' He disappeared into the cockpit again and was back almost immediately, a small black wooden box in his arms. Lifting the lid he peered inside then with the air of a conjuror producing a rabbit from a hat he proceeded to lift the contents of the box for everyone to see.

'One tin of tomato soup. One packet of digestive biscuits. One tin of vegetable soup. One packet of Garibaldi biscuits. . .'

'Very emergency rations. . .' muttered Paul who had followed William into the aircraft and was standing watching Henry.

'Better than charcoaled snake,' observed Hilary.

'What do you mean, charcoaled snake?' Ruth's voice was shrill.

'Well, it could come to that if the Garibaldi run out,' said Hilary drily.

'What else have you got there?' Toni, who had been watching Henry, had noticed his expression change as he peered once more into the bottom of the box.

'Just one other thing. . .' he replied, and slowly drew

out a pistol, which he held up for everyone to see.

There was silence in the cabin.

'Lutas covered every eventuality,' said Jack at last.

'I suppose if he was attacked by some wild animal he would have no option but to use it,' observed Paul uneasily.

'Not only animals,' replied William.

'What do you mean?' demanded Ruth, and Toni heard the note of hysteria in her voice.

'There has been much ivory-poaching lately in the region—much looting—bad men, desperate men. Lutas protect himself.' William nodded at the pistol.

Ruth gave a little moan and as if on cue, as if he knew he was being discussed, Lutas stirred.

Jack glanced down at him. 'I want to get his wounds stitched,' he muttered. 'Could you sort some dressings out, Toni?'

She nodded and turned to the medical supplies that were stacked in one corner.

'How will you see, Jack?' asked Henry. 'It's almost dark.'

'There's one flashlight in the cabin,' replied Jack; 'I hope to God the battery lasts. William, could you light the fire? We'll move Lutas into the doorway, then the firelight will help as well.'

Toni fumbled around in the gloom and in the stack of medical supplies found dressing packs, antiseptic lotion, local anaesthetic and surgical gloves.

By the time they had moved Lutas into the doorway William had lit the fire and the light from the flames illuminated the whole area. Henry held the flashlight directly above Lutas's injured legs then switched off the beam until Jack was ready to start.

'It's all very primitive,' said Toni, 'you can't even wash your hands, but at least you have these.' She handed him the surgical gloves.

He eased them over his hands. 'We're lucky really,' he said. 'If we hadn't been carrying these supplies it would have been a lot more primitive. Would you draw up a shot of Lignocaine? Lucas is still pretty well sedated but if he should come round that should take the sting out of it.'

Henry switched on the flash and for one moment in the circle of light, as Jack leaned over his patient and the faces of the other receded into the darkness of the aircraft, Toni was reminded of pictures she'd seen of field stations in war with medics operating under appalling conditions.

Then, images and impressions forgotten, she too pulled on a pair of surgical gloves and drew up the Lignocaine. While Jack administered the drug into the swollen flesh Toni soaked cotton wool swabs with antiseptic solution then cleansed the wounds.

Henry held the lamp steady and Hilary wiped Lutas's face with cologne impregnated tissues she'd found in Ruth's luggage when she'd been looking for food.

The wounds were deep where jagged pieces of metal had dug into the flesh, and in places they gaped wide, revealing the bone beneath.

Jack had already set the bones into the makeshift splints as best he could, but as he carefully began to suture the wounds, drawing the flesh firmly together, Toni could sense that he had grave doubts as to the outcome of what he was doing.

As if he could read her thoughts he glanced up and, as his eyes met hers, he said, 'The left tibia is shattered—and the right fibula may be fractured, I'm not sure. I can't do much—he needs X-rays and surgery.'

She sensed the helpless desperation in his voice. 'You're doing everything possible in the circumstances,' she murmured.

He worked on in silence, the only sounds the crackling and hissing as William threw more wood on to the fire, and the far off cry of some animal deep in the bush.

Intently Toni watched as Jack's strong fingers worked, probing, stabbing the needle and drawing the thread. The wing of his hair had fallen forward over his forehead and gleamed like gold in the lamplight. Deep shadows cast by the strange light threw his features into sharp relief, the curved nose and the hollows beneath his cheekbones again reminding Toni of some bird of prey.

After what seemed an eternity he flung down the needle and sat back on his heels.

'That's it,' he said. 'I can't do more.'

Toni moved forward and began tidying up and applying dressings as with a deep sigh Jack peeled off his gloves.

'Were there antibiotics in the supplies?' he asked suddenly.

Toni shook her head. 'Afraid not. I already looked.'

'There should have been.' Jack frowned. 'I ordered some.'

'Well, there aren't any there. I'll check again if you like.'

'Don't bother. The suppliers aren't very reliable—it wouldn't be the first time they've let me down.' He sighed and drew a hand wearily over his face, fingering the dark stubble on his chin.

Toni was suddenly struck by just how fatigued he looked.

He glanced across at her, saw her watching him and pushed back his hair, as he did so revealing the livid line of the cut on his forehead.

Toni frowned and leaned forward. 'I think while we're at it, Jack,' she said boldly, 'you'd better let me stitch that cut for you.'

For one moment she thought he was going to refuse, then Henry suddenly leaned forward and intervened.

'Good idea,' he said, 'but could you get a move on? This battery isn't going to last for ever.'

Rapidly Toni donned a clean pair of surgical gloves and opened another dressing pack while Jack sat against the edge of the plane's open doorway, leaned his head back and with a sigh closed his eyes.

She was about to draw up another shot of Lignocaine when he opened one eye. 'Save that,' he said quietly, 'we may be glad of it.'

'But it will sting,' she warned.

He closed his eyes again. 'Just get on with it.'

She glanced at Henry, who gave a helpless shrug, hesitated for only another moment, then taking a deep breath she threaded the needle and crawling forward in the confined space prepared a swab and cleansed the cut.

He flinched only once when she inserted the first suture; after that the only indication he gave of pain was the slight flaring of his nostrils and his hands clenched into fists by his side, the knuckles strained and showing white in the light from the lamp.

Without suturing, the cut would undoubtedly have left a scar.

When Toni had finished she sat back and critically surveyed her handiwork. 'There you are, Dr Christy,' she said when she was satisfied she'd done the best she could, 'you'll do.'

As if he'd been holding his breath, Jack let it go in a long sigh, then he opened one eye and looked at her.

'There aren't,' he said sardonically, 'too many women I'd allow to put me through what you just have.'

'Sorry.' She grinned. 'I did warn you.'

'Forget it.' He pulled a face then suddenly, unexpectedly, as she had been about to turn away, he touched her arm.

She paused, froze for a moment then allowed her eyes to meet his. 'What is it?'

'Thanks.' He said it so softly that not even Henry, who was still fiddling with the lamp, heard, then as her heart leapt uncomfortably, he added, 'Dr Nash.'

It was more than gratitude, it was the final acceptance of her position, a position that had been in doubt between them ever since he had voiced his preference for a male medical assistant.

'Think nothing of it,' she replied. 'All in a day's work.' She tried to sound casual but found that her pulse was racing. In spite of the urgency of the situation and their mutual professional standing there had been something deeply intimate about the act she had just performed. Even as she struggled with the sudden intensity of her feelings, the lamp flickered and went out, leaving them only with the glow of the fire.

'Well, that's that,' said Henry. 'What do we do now?'

'I suggest,' said Jack, 'that we divide the rations, have something to eat and drink, then try and get some rest.'

'Thank goodness for that,' called Paul from the interior of the cabin. 'I'm starving.'

The biscuits, the drop of soup and the water could have done little to alleviate Paul's hunger, but he didn't complain and afterwards they all donned jumpers and jackets and tried to make themselves as comfortable as possible to pass the long hours of the night.

Toni didn't think she would sleep but she must have done, because she came to with a start and realised she had been dreaming.

She had been outside in the street and it was snowing, icy-cold, and she was only dressed in T-shirt and shorts.

She was still cold, shivering, and she lay in the darkness wondering where she was. In her room at the hospital a street-light shone through the window. There was no street-light here.

Then she remembered.

She turned her head and heard Hilary's even breathing beside her, Ruth's restless mutterings. Her shivering grew worse and carefully, so as not to disturb Hilary, she got up and moved down the cabin.

As she passed Diaka she paused and peered down at the girl, whose profile was just discernible in the faint light from the doorway. The girl slept peacefully—it was the first time Toni had seen her out of control, utterly defenceless in sleep. As she watched Diaka, Toni's teeth started to chatter and she quickly moved on, afraid now of disturbing the others.

She paused when she reached the doorway and saw that the fire still glowed brightly.

A figure sat hunched in front of it and soundlessly Toni sat in the doorway and slid out of the plane.

It wasn't until she reached the figure and he lifted his head that she realised it was Jack.

'Couldn't you sleep?' he asked, staring up at her.

'I have s-slept, but I'm so c-cold.' She crouched down and held out her hands to the remains of the fire. 'I c-can't seem to s-s-top shaking.'

He moved then, stood up and threw the last of the packing cases on to the fire.

She watched gratefully as the fire burst into life again and tiny blue flames began licking the edges of the wood. Then she felt Jack drape something round her shoulders and, glancing round, she realised it was his own bush jacket.

'It's all r-right,' she chattered. 'You'll g-get c-c-cold.'

'You're in shock,' he said abruptly. 'We must get you warm.'

Still she shivered and shook and was beginning to feel quite faint when she felt Jack push her head between her knees.

When the mists in her head finaly began to recede he pushed her back so that she was lying on the ground.

The next thing she knew he was lying almost on top of her, the weight of his body pinning her to the ground.

Instinctively she began to struggle. What the hell was he doing? How dared he take advantage of her?

Then she heard his voice in her ear.

'Stop struggling.' It was a command, and the authority in his tone made her obey instantly. 'I have to get you warm. This is the only choice left.'

She fell silent as she felt his arms go around her, drawing her close so that almost immediately she felt the warmth from his own body. She was vaguely aware that he had pulled his bush jacket so that it covered them both and he had eased the pair of them close enough to the fire so that they could feel the heat from the flames on their faces.

At first she simply stopped struggling as the fight went out of her, but still she clung to the front edges of his shirt, then gradually, as the warmth began to creep back into her body, she relaxed, lost her grip on his shirt and simply lay still in the warm cocoon he had created.

At last her shivering ceased and with a deep sigh she closed her eyes.

This time she dreamt she was at home with her mother. Once again they had been shopping, only this time they had been in a supermarket, shopping for food—joints of meat, succulent chickens, bread, fruit, wine. . .but then, when they reached the checkout, the cashier was Jack Christy who told them they had to eat all the food before they left the store.

She awoke laughing, attempted to turn over, but found herself imprisoned, then realised with a start that she was still lying in Jack Christy's arms, that the fire had burnt right down and that Jack was awake and was watching her, his face only inches from her own.

'You slept,' he said softly.

'Yes.' She gave up the attempt to move, content for the moment to remain drowsy, in the warmth and safety of his arms.

'Are you feeling better?'

'I think so. I'm certainly warm again.'

'It was shock.'

'Yes, I suppose it was. It started soon after the crash—I remember I was trembling, then I was so busy I forgot about it and I guess it got delayed.'

'The worst kind.' He shifted slightly and she felt the hardness of his thigh-bone grind against hers.

She thought, maybe, she really should move, but before she could do anything her attention was taken by a movement from the plane.

A figure, unmistakably Henry's even in the half-light, appeared in the doorway, paused, jumped to the ground and stumbled. He swore softly under his breath then ambled off in the direction of the latrine.

'He's been a tower of strength,' she said quietly.

Jack didn't answer, and she turned her head slightly to look at him. The sharpness of his profile was finely etched against the sky already lightening with the impending dawn. 'It's the most unexpected people who come up trumps in a crisis,' she added at last.

'You didn't do so badly yourself, from what I've heard,' he murmured.

'You said that as if you hadn't expected me to either,' she said ruefully, then before he had the chance to reply, whether to deny or confirm her veiled accusation, she said, 'Go on, admit it, you thought I was pretty useless, didn't you?'

He took a deep breath. 'I must confess, I had my doubts.'

'I still don't understand why. My training. . .'

'It had nothing to do with your training. . .it was purely and simply because you are a woman. . .'

'Ah, sexist in the extreme. . .'

'Not that, either. . .you quite obviously do your job as well as, if not better than, some men I know. . .'

'Then what. . .?'

He didn't answer as Henry suddenly lurched back into the clearing, caught sight of them, stopped and peered at them through half-light. He then raised his hand and continued on his way back to the aircraft as if it was the most natural thing in the world to have found them lying on the ground in front of the fire, locked in each other's arms.

'It's purely,' he said at last as Henry disappeared, 'a question of physical strength and stamina—as I told you before, I speak from experience. Other women we've had out here rarely stay the course— maybe it's the climate, or the conditions—I just don't know.'

'Perhaps I shall surprise you.'

'Perhaps you will,' he agreed, then softly added, 'little thing that you are.' Involuntarily he tightened his grip and she felt her pulse quicken. It was a long time since she'd lain in a man's arms. . .but Jack Christy felt very different from Martin Foster. But then he would; the reason she was in Jack Christy's arms was a different one entirely. . .but it felt good all the same. Maybe, she told herself, she had a fever and was starting to hallucinate.

They remained silent for a long while.

'I wonder what today will bring forth,' said Jack at last.

'You think the authorities might find us today?' she asked hopefully.

'They might.' He hesitated. 'That is, if they've missed us yet.'

'Don't you think they would?' She half turned her head in surprise.

'I don't know. . .don't forget we were supposed to be travelling to Jabhati by road, which would have taken longer anyway. . .'

'But surely Lutas would have had to give some notice of his flight, time of arrival. . .that sort of thing.'

'One would have thought so. . .'

'You mean he may not. . .?'

'Lutas was a bit lax about things like that. But don't say anything to the others. . .it's probably better for all of us if Ruth thinks the Tanzanian emergency services are actually roaring to the rescue.'

'Jack, how long can we survive?' she asked after a while.

She felt rather than saw the shrug of his shoulders. 'We have enough water for about two or three days. After that, we'll have to think again. . .but let's hope it won't get that far. For the moment we sit tight.'

As Jack spoke, the tall figure of William loped into the clearing from the direction of the belt of thorn trees. He nodded at them then headed for the aircraft.

'Where did he sleep?' asked Toni.

'Who knows?' Jack stretched, and Toni eased her cramped muscles and groaned. 'You did sleep, didn't you?' he asked.

'Surprisingly, yes. I dreamt I was at home shopping with my mother; we were buying food, lots of food.'

'Where is home, Toni?' He had sat forward and was rubbing his ankles but he turned his head to look back at her.

Suddenly she felt bereft and wanted him to put his arms around her again. Maybe it was the mention of home that had done it.

She swallowed but her throat felt dry, gritty. 'Chichester,' she said shortly, then, unable to go on as all sorts of images of home began to form in her mind's eye, she attempted to be flippant.

'How would you like me to cook breakfast, Dr Christy?'

'What did you have in mind?' he asked drily.

'How about bacon, eggs, mushrooms, kidneys?'

He shook his head. 'I'd much prefer grilled Garibaldi.' With a wry smile he climbed stiffly to his feet, reaching out to assist her.

His hand, warm and dry, encircled hers, and in that instant she knew that, whatever horrors they might still have to face, she could cope, provided this man was by her side.

CHAPTER SEVEN

DAYLIGHT came rapidly, dispersing the soft purplish haze that had settled over the bush and flooding the landscape with the bright, almost blinding light that was Africa.

Dozens of tiny, vividly coloured birds rose in swarms from the thorn trees where they had spent the night, and from the top of the rockface the vultures rose again and began their relentless circling.

The other passengers began to stir, then to complain as they stretched stiffened limbs. The braver among them headed for the latrine. Hilary bullied Ruth into sharing her impregnated tissues and bottle of mouthwash so that everyone could at least make some attempt to freshen up.

Then while Toni dispensed biscuits Hilary filled drinking containers, and everyone, with the exception of Lutas, came out of the plane and sat on the ground around the still glowing embers of the fire.

Even Ruth came, nursing her injured arm in the sling that Toni had applied, and Diaka, quiet and watchful.

They breakfasted in silence.

It took almost no time at all but, long after the last crumb had been devoured, the last drop of water drunk, still they sat there.

It was Henry who spoke first, Henry, who looked old and grey, exhausted, after the previous day's ordeal.

NO RISK, NO OBLIGATION TO BUY...NOW OR EVER!

CASINO JUBILEE

"Scratch'n Match" Game
Here's how to play:

1. Peel off label from front cover. Place it in the space provided opposite. With a coin carefully scratch away the silver box. This makes you eligible to receive two or more free books, and possibly another gift, depending upon what is revealed beneath the scratch-off area.

2. Send back this card and you'll receive specially selected Love on Call novels. These books have a cover price of £1.80* each, but they are yours to keep absolutely free.

3. There's no catch. You're under no obligation to buy anything. We charge nothing for your first shipment. And you don't have to make any minimum number of purchases - not even one!

4. The fact is thousands of readers enjoy receiving books by mail from Mills & Boon Reader Service, at least a month before they're available in the shops. They like the convenience of home delivery, and there is no extra charge for postage and packing.

5. We hope that after receiving your free books you'll want to remain a subscriber. But the choice is yours - to continue or cancel, anytime at all! So why not take up our invitation, with no risk of any kind. You'll be glad you did!

*Prices subject to change without notice.

YOURS FREE!

This cute fluffy duck with its soft yellow down and adorable expression is sure to delight you - and it's yours absolutely free - when you accept our offer.

CASINO JUBILEE
"Scratch'n Match" Game

SCRATCH HERE ?

PLACE LABEL HERE

CHECK CLAIM CHART BELOW FOR YOUR FREE GIFTS!

YES! I have placed my label from the front cover in the space provided above and scratched away the silver box. Please send me all the gifts for which I qualify. I understand that I am under no obligation to purchase any books, as explained on the back and on the opposite page. I am over 18 years of age.

MS/MRS/MISS/MR _____   1A5D

ADDRESS _____

_____

————————— POSTCODE —————————

CASINO JUBILEE CLAIM CHART

🍒🍒🍒	**WORTH 4 FREE BOOKS A FREE FLUFFY DUCK AND MYSTERY GIFT**	
🍒🔔🍒	**WORTH 4 FREE BOOKS**	
🔔🍒🍒	**WORTH 3 FREE BOOKS**	CLAIM Nº 1,528

Mills & Boon Reader Service
FREEPOST
P.O. Box 70
Croydon
Surrey
CR9 9EL

NO
STAMP
NEEDED

'I've been thinking,' he said, and they all looked up, aroused from their own thoughts by the sound of his voice. 'Shouldn't we be trying to do something?'

'What do you suggest?' It was Jack who answered.

'I don't know really.' Henry shrugged. 'I just thought maybe one or two of us should perhaps explore, even try to go for help. . . Maybe all of us should move. . .I don't know.'

'And how long do you think we would last in the open bush with no supplies, no shelter and only one pistol?' asked Jack.

'I don't know.' Henry shrugged again.

'I know what Henry means,' said Paul suddenly. 'I feel so helpless just sitting doing nothing—surely there's something we could do?'

'I can assure you we are better off staying put,' replied Jack grimly. 'For a start, even though the plane is partly in the trees there is a good chance it will be spotted from the air by any rescue party—a group of people on foot in the bush would just merge into the landscape and be totally unidentifiable.

'Also,' he went on when the others remained silent, 'the plane is shelter, protection—which we wouldn't have in the open.' He paused and glanced round at each of them. 'The other thing you're forgetting is that we have an injured man in our party who would have to be carried, and we also have a pregnant woman.'

Instinctively they all glanced at Diaka, who, sensing that she was being discussed, lowered her eyes in embarrassment.

'So for the moment——' Jack scrambled to his feet

'—we carry on as we are and hope it won't be too long before someone finds us.'

Watched by the others, he began to walk towards the plane, then he slowed and looked over his shoulder. 'Toni, would you give me a hand to change Lutas's dressings please?' he called.

She climbed stiffly to her feet and was about to follow Jack into the plane when she became aware of the continuing silence from the others.

'Oh, come on, you lot,' she said, looking round at the ring of gloomy faces, 'do buck up. At least we are all alive. It's another glorious day——' she threw her arms wide and lifted her face to the sun which in spite of the earliness of the hour already felt warm '—people pay thousands of pounds to go on safari in the bush, and here we are with it offered to us on a plate. For goodness' sake let's enjoy it, even if there is nothing else on the plate.'

'Toni's right.' Hilary too hauled herself to her feet. 'We're an ungrateful lot. It could all have been so much worse. We could have all been killed, or some of us could have been, in which case the rest of us would have been trying to bury the others at this point in time. As it is, all we have to do is lounge around in the sun waiting to be picked up—and that can't be long. This is the 1990s, for God's sake, not the Dark Ages!'

With a smile of relief Toni hurried on to the plane amid mutterings from the others as, shamed by her cajoling and Hilary's outburst, they began sorting themselves out.

The air was stale in the comparative dimness of the

plane and Toni paused, narrowing her eyes, trying to adjust to the lack of light. Jack was crouching beside Lutas, who appeared to be awake. He glanced up at her as she approached.

'I'll try and make him more comfortable,' he said. 'You get some clean dressings.'

She nodded and edged her way to the rear of the plane and the pile of medical supplies now minus their packing cases. She found a fresh dressing pack and a packet of disposable syringes. When she got back to Lutas she found that Jack had used the empty soup tin as a urinal for the injured man.

'I'll just get rid of this,' he said, standing up. 'Do you have any more of those wipes, to sponge his face? Just as well you don't shave, old man.' He grinned down at Lutas who managed a faint smile in return. 'We couldn't oblige there.'

While Jack disappeared outside, Toni knelt beside Lutas.

'Hello,' she said, 'how are you feeling?'

He raised his eyes to hers. 'Never felt better,' he answered bravely through lips that were already cracked and dry.

Carefully she wiped his bronzed, weathered face, squeezing every drop of the precious moisture from the wipe, then, lifting his head and supporting the back of his neck with one hand, she held the plastic container so that he could drink his water ration.

He drank noisily, greedily, looking for more when he had finished, then while Toni busied herself with removing his dressings he followed her with his eyes.

'Where is everyone?' he asked at last.

'They're all outside,' she answered, her gaze flickering briefly to the door.

'All alive?'

'Yes, Lutas, all alive,' she replied firmly, then added, 'thanks to you.'

He grunted, then gave a great sigh and leaned his head back. He remained silent while she opened the dressing pack then, as if it had just occurred to him, he said, 'The young fellow, is he OK?'

'You mean Paul?' She paused and glanced at him.

'The asthmatic.'

'Yes, he's fine.'

'But he had no medication.'

'I know, but believe it or not he's been the least of our troubles.'

He frowned. 'The others. . .?'

'Ruth—Mrs Galloway. . .she dislocated her shoulder in the landing—we've put her right now, but well, to be honest, Lutas,' she smiled, 'you've been our biggest concern, and Diaka of course.'

She could have bitten out her tongue the moment she said it but to her relief Lutas didn't seem to have noticed, and at that moment Jack returned and the moment passed.

Jack donned a pair of surgical gloves and carefully examined Lutas's injuries.

'They're doing very nicely,' he said at last. 'I think I made a good job of that particular piece of needlework, even if I do say so myself.'

'What about the breaks?' Lutas pulled a face then winced with pain.

'Can't speak for those, I'm afraid,' replied Jack. 'In

the lap of the gods—like the rest of us at the moment,' he added grimly.

'Should be someone looking for us soon,' muttered Lutas, his body beginning to twitch with renewed pain.

Toni took the clean dressings from the pack and carefully covered the wounds with the gauze dressing pads.

'I'll give you another shot of morphine, Lutas,' said Jack, taking a syringe from the packet and an ampoule of Papaveretum from his medical bag.

'Just a minute. . .' Lutas gasped, stetching one hand urgently out to Jack. 'Stay put, won't you?'

'What do you mean?' Jack was about to draw up the injection but he paused and stared down at Lutas, who was beginning to twist and writhe with the pain.

'Stay near the plane. . .don't let anyone wander off. . .'

'No, I've already made that quite clear,' replied Jack firmly.

'Water. . .?'

'It's been rationed. . .enough for a couple of days.'

'Good. . .should be here by then.' Lutas sighed again and closed his eyes as if the effort had all been too much. He remained silent while Jack administered the morphine and Toni secured the dressings with surgical tape.

He opened his eyes once more, before the blessed oblivion of the drug claimed him again, and looked at Jack. 'The Masai girl?' he mumbled.

'Diaka? Yes, what about her?'

Lutas's gaze flickered to Toni, who lowered her eyes in embarrassment. Jack turned to her and she realised she had to give some explanation.

'Sorry,' she murmured, quietly so that Lutas couldn't hear. 'I let it slip we were concerned about her—but I didn't say why,' she added hastily.

Jack sighed and turned back to Lutas, but before he had the chance to offer any explanation the pilot said. 'She's expecting, isn't she?'

'How did you know. . .?'

'I didn't, I've just twigged. . .if I had known you wouldn't have got away with it, Christy, you old devil—you'll get me shot,' he muttered.

'That's why I didn't tell you—I knew you wouldn't take her if you knew. I figured what you didn't know. . .sorry, old man. I had to get her back. . .it's a pretty desperate story.'

The mists claimed Lutas then and Toni remained silent, clearing away the soiled dressings. At last she threw Jack an apprehensive glance.

'Sorry,' she said. 'I let it out without thinking.'

'It's OK.' He shook his head. 'It's a wonder any of us can think straight. Besides, Lutas would probably have found out anyway.'

She hesitated, then unable to contain her curiosity, said, 'What did you mean when you said Diaka's was a pretty desperate story?'

'Just that.'

'She's from Jabhati?'

'Yes.'

'So what was she doing in Nairobi?'

'It's the old story, I'm afraid.' As he spoke, Jack absent mindedly began winding a bandage round his fingers. 'Her parents had refused to allow her to marry the boy she loves. When she found she was pregnant, she didn't tell anyone—not even the boy, who would have faced punishment—she ran away so as not to bring shame onto both their families.'

'Would she have been allowed to marry him if they'd known of her pregnancy?' asked Toni curiously.

'That's debatable.' Jack pulled a face. 'Diaka's father is an important man in Jabhati and he had already arranged a marriage between his daughter and an elder from another village—a man of sixty-two.'

Toni gave a slight shudder. 'So how did you know she was in Nairobi?'

'I didn't. It was sheer chance. She'd walked from Jabhati to Arusha then hitched a lift in a farmer's truck to Nairobi. She'd heard stories about Nairobi and thought she could find work there to support herself and the baby. Unfortunately almost as soon as she arrived she was attacked and raped and her few possessions were stolen. I saw her quite by chance; she was begging on the street outside the Jacaranda Hotel. She'd been making just enough to stay in that shack you saw. I finally managed to persuade her to return to Jabhati with me.'

'What about her parents? How will they react?'

'With relief, I suspect. They were devastated when they discovered she'd gone. They imagine she must be dead by now. The boy wanted to go and find her but he has to work to support his elderly father.'

'And the man of sixty-two?'

'He was so angry at being humiliated that he married a girl from another villiage in retaliation—she was only thirteen, I believe.'

'They have such strange customs,' said Toni slowly.

'You'll have to get used to their ways,' said Jack, but this time there was no scorn in his voice.

'I know,' she sighed, 'it's just that some things seem so hard.'

'It works both ways, you know.' He grinned suddenly.

'What do you mean?' She threw him a curious glance.

'They will think you strange as well.'

'Why?'

'Because you are unmarried—at, what—how old are you?' He narrowed his eyes and stared at her. 'Twenty-six?'

'Yes. . .but. . .'

'They will think that very strange, believe me. . .all those wasted childbearing years.'

'I've never thought of it like that. . .' She turned away from the glint of amusement in his grey eyes, as to her dismay she felt her cheeks redden.

'Haven't you?' he said softly. 'Have you never wanted children?'

'Well, yes, I guess one day I would like them, but my career has always. . .'

'So you've never loved a man enought to want to have his child?' he went on relentlessly.

Suddenly she was aware that he had moved in very close behind her, and as she felt the warmth of his breath on the back of her neck she was reminded again of the hours of the night when he had held her closely and warmed her with his own body. . .

'Haven't you, Toni?' he murmured in her ear.

'Haven't you ever wanted anyone that much? Has there never been anyone?'

'Well, yes, of course there has.' Stung now by his implication that she had always been unloved, she felt goaded into retaliation. 'Yes, as a matter of fact there was someone once,' she added defiantly.

'Ah,' he breathed, 'I thought as much. . .someone serious?'

'Yes, someone serious, very serious,' she snapped.

'So what happened?'

'It didn't work out, that's all.'

'So he's not around now—this man who meant so much?'

'No. No, he isn't around now, at least not in that way,' she added, suddenly furious with herself for feeling she had to explain.

'Is that why you came to Africa—to get over it, to forget him?'

'No, it wasn't!' Angrily she pulled away and turned to face him. 'It was over between Martin and myself a long time ago.'

'Oh, so it was Martin, was it?' A smile flickered across his features. 'Was he a doctor too?'

'No, if you must know, he's a teacher.'

'Oh, a teacher! So what did he think about this jaunt of yours to the wild continent?'

'Actually he thinks I'm mad—but I've already told you it was over long before I even thought——'

She was interrupted by a shout of laughter from Jack. 'He thinks you're mad? You know something? He's probably right. We must all be mad to want to spend our lives in a place like Jabhati.'

'Is that what Shakira thinks as well?' Boldly she asked the question, saw him stop in surprise, saw his eyes narrow at mention of the woman whom he was to marry.

Then as she too recalled Shakira and her dark, voluptuous beauty, for the first time Toni became conscious of her own appearance, of the fact that not only was she not wearing make-up, but she hadn't bathed or changed her clothes and that in the heat her hair was sticking unattractively to her head and neck.

To add to her growing discomfort Jack continued to stare at her, but she was saved from further embarrassment by a series of ear-splitting screams that suddenly rent the air.

Startled, they stared at each other in alarm.

'What the hell. . .?' Jack automatically dived for the open doorway.

'Ruth. . .?' Toni followed him, stumbling over someone's rucksack as she went and banging her knee on the sharp edge of one of the seats.

But it wasn't Ruth. As Toni paused in the doorway and looked round she saw to her surprise that it was Hilary, the usually calm, level-headed Hilary who was standing, white-faced with shock, staring at Lutas's wooden box that she had used as a supply store.

William, who apparently had gone to investigate her distress, was crouching over the box.

He glanced up, a broad grin on his usually serious face as Toni and Jack scrambled from the aircraft and hurried towards him.

'What is it?' asked Jack. 'A snake?'

'No,' William laughed, shaking his head, 'just a spider.'

'Just a spider!' yelled Hilary. 'Just a spider, he says. It was the biggest bloody spider I've ever seen in my life.' She turned helplessly to Toni and clutched her arm. 'Honestly, Toni, it was as big as the palm of my hand—and hairy—uggh! Thick black hairs and it moved so fast—God only knows where it went.'

'It's OK, Hilary,' said Jack reassuringly as he peered into the box. 'It's gone now, scuttled away in fright when you screamed at it, I shouldn't wonder.' He grinned. 'That was a scream to chill the blood, you know.'

'I'm sorry,' Hilary muttered. She still clutched Toni's arm but was beginning to look shamefaced. 'I've always been afraid of spiders—they scare me to death when they run so fast.'

'I thought it might have been a snake,' said Jack, straightening up. 'Always check before you sit down anywhere, won't you?' He glanced at the others who had gathered to see what the commotion was about. 'Oh, and while we're on the subject, if you take your shoes off, make sure you look inside them before you put them on again.'

'Scorpion,' said William. 'Nasty,' he said simply.

'Very nasty,' added Jack.

Ruth shuddered. 'I'm beginning to hate this country,' she complained.

'Oh, I don't know,' said Paul, 'it's very beautiful as well. Did you see that lizard sunning itself over there just now? It was the most gorgeous colour.'

'I think I could forgo that experience and swap it for a bath and a clean bed,' said Ruth sourly. 'Where do you think those rescue services have got to, Dr Christy?'

'I'm sure they are on their way, Mrs Galloway,' replied Jack pleasantly. 'But in the meantime I suggest we prepare ourselves for the possibility of another day, and maybe a night in the bush. For a start we need more wood for the fire—Paul? Henry?' He glanced at the other men as he spoke and they nodded. 'And William, maybe you could give me a hand to shovel more earth into the latrine?'

'Sure, Doctor.' William smiled his lazy smile.

Jack nodded then looked at Hilary. 'All right now?' he asked and his tone wasn't without sympathy.

'Yes, thanks, Jack.' The hysteria had gone from her voice and she looked calm again. 'Sorry about that, I'm fine now.'

'Don't worry about it; we all have our own personal demons.' Jack narrowed his eyes against the sun which was already growing fierce. 'Supplies going OK?' he added casually.

'Yes—going being the operative word.' Hilary grimaced. 'I'll open the other tin of soup today. I wish we had something to supplement it.' She glanced round. 'Do you think we could risk any roots or berries?'

'Best not,' replied Jack. 'At least——' he hesitated and looked over his shoulder at Ruth, saw she wasn't within earshot and added '—not unless we are forced to—they could cause all sorts of tummy gripes, and we don't have the liquid to cope with dehydration.'

As Jack moved away with the other men Hilary turned to Toni and pulled a face. 'I feel such a twit,' she said.

'Don't be silly—I would have probably done the same thing,' admitted Toni. 'I'm not too keen on spiders either, if the truth be known. I hate it at home in the autumn when those huge black spiders come indoors.'

'You didn't seem too worried about spiders last night.'

Toni had been about to go back to the plane but she stopped in her tracks and stared at Hilary.

'Whatever do you mean?' she asked, but already the expression on Hilary's face gave her an inkling what the other girl was thinking.

Hilary's next words confirmed her suspicion. 'Well, I wouldn't have thought the ground was the best place to be lying if one doesn't like spiders. . .on the other hand, of course, if one has a hunky man to protect one, maybe it doesn't matter. . .'

'I don't know what you're talking about,' muttered Toni indignantly but she could feel her cheeks growing warm.

'Don't tell me I dreamt it!' Hilary's eyes widened innocently. 'Or maybe after all that excitement yesterday I was hallucinating. Do you know, Toni, I could have sworn when I got up in the night to have a pee that you and Jack Christy were lying in each other's arms, right there in front of the fire? Dead romantic, that's what I thought at the time. . .now you're telling me I imagined it.'

'I didn't say you were imagining it,' protested Toni.

'Oh, so you really were having a cuddle?'

'No!' she cried, then, as Hilary raised her eyebrows, she said, but more quietly this time, 'No, Hilary we weren't, as you put it, having a cuddle. Jack was merely trying to warm me up——'

'Where I come from that was always known as having a cuddle.'

'I was suffering from delayed shock. . .'

'I bet you were.' Hilary grinned. 'So would I be if I spent the night in Jack Christy's arms.'

'No, you don't understand—you've got it all wrong,' protested Toni, then, as Hilary continued grinning, she snapped, 'Besides what were you doing going to the loo on your own? Jack said we had to go to the latrine accompanied by someone.'

'Who would you have suggested?' Hilary asked coolly. 'Ruth was moaning, Diaka was totally unapproachable. Lutas was out for the count. Henry was snoring his head off, there was no sign of William, and Paul—well, if I'd gone with Paul I wouldn't have been certain who would have been protecting who.'

'Even so. . .'

'I must admit,' Hilary went on relentlessly, 'when I awoke, you, Toni, were my first choice, but I couldn't find you: then, when I decided to brave the horrors of the night on my own, I saw for myself that you were otherwise engaged. I wasn't sure just what you were doing, but I didn't fancy incurring Jack Christy's wrath by interrupting anything, so I simply crept by.'

'You went all the way to the latrine on your own?' By this time, in spite of herself, Toni was laughing.

'Well, no, not exactly,' Hilary admitted. 'I crouched down behind the nearest thorn bush. Then some animal started snuffling around behind me and I scarpered back to the plane as fast as I could go. . .and let's face it, Toni, you and Jack didn't even know I'd passed you, did you?'

'No,' Toni grinned. 'No, we didn't. . . at least, I didn't; Jack may have done. . .'

'Do you think,' Hilary mused, 'tonight, if I were to say I was cold, he would do the same for me?'

'Hilary, it really wasn't what you thought.' Toni sighed and began walking back to the plane again while Hilary, after picking up the box of supplies and peering suspiciously inside, fell into step beside her.

'I'm glad to hear it,' Hilary replied.

Suddenly Toni realised the humour and joking were over and Hilary had grown serious. Before she could comment, however, Hilary went on, 'He's spoken for, Toni. I'd hate to see you get hurt.'

'Don't worry,' she replied firmly, 'there's absolutely no fear of that.' By this time they had reached the plane and Toni stood aside for Hilary to precede her.

'Good. Just don't forget it.' Hilary nodded and climbed into the plane ahead of her.

CHAPTER EIGHT

THERE really weren't any grounds for Hilary's concern, Toni told herself firmly, as a little later, she rummaged through her luggage to find herself a clean T-shirt. No matter what interpretation Hilary might have put on what she'd seen the night before, Toni knew her conscience was clear.

Jack Christy had quite simply been treating her for shock.

Besides, wasn't she right off men at the present time?

Since her relationship with Martin had ended she had avoided becoming involved again, deliberately channelling all her energies into her career.

And even if she had been looking for romance, she would hardly have looked in Jack Christy's direction. As Hilary had taken pains to point out, and as she had been only too aware, he was indeed spoken for. The image of the exotic Shakira seemed to shimmer like some mirage in the white hot sky, a reminder that she was the woman Jack was to marry.

But what, some little demon niggled at the back of her mind, if he weren't spoken for? What if he were a free man? Would she be interested then? She was, after all, only human, and very few women could deny that Jack Christy was a very attractive man.

Her thoughts inevitably turned to the hours she'd spent locked in his arms, where in spite of her shock and discomfort from the cold she had been only too aware of the strength of him, the hardness of his body. . . Would she be interested in him in normal circumstances? Was he the type of man who would appeal to her?

When she'd first met him she hadn't really liked him, had thought him arrogant, chauvinistic. . .but since then she'd seen another side to him. . .

Angrily she shook herself. The questions were purely hypothetical. She had things to do. The quicker she put all thoughts of Jack Christy, or any other man for that matter, firmly out of her mind, the better.

Speedily she ripped off her soiled shirt and pulled a clean T-shirt over her head, then, taking a comb from her rucksack, she combed the tangles from her hair.

When she had finished she walked to the doorway where she stood for a moment bracing herself before going out into the heat of the sun again, then she realised that Jack was holding some sort of meeting.

He glanced up at her as she stood there and his gaze flickered over her as if it registered with him that she had changed her shirt, made an attempt to tidy herself.

But that was ridiculous, Jack Christy would never notice anything like that, and even if he had it wouldn't mean anything to him. Toni climbed down and walked towards the others, noticing as she did so an air of excitement about them.

'What is it?' she asked, looking round. 'Has something happened?'

'Henry has been getting some sort of reception from the radio,' said Jack. He spoke quietly but even he looked excited.

'But that's marvellous—well done, Henry!' Toni turned impulsively to the older man who nodded with pleasure.

'Don't get too excited,' he said cautiously, 'it was only a few crackles.'

'But it's the best we've had so far.' Paul began to hop about.

'We were just saying before you came out,' said Jack to Toni, 'that we ought to try and get some idea of our bearings. If we can pick up someone on the radio we want to be able to give them an idea where they can look for us. I'm going to scout around a bit.'

'Lutas said to stay put. . .' Toni began dubiously.

'I know, I won't go far.' Jack stood up. 'William will come with me and we'll take Lutas's pistol with us.' He paused and looked round, his gaze coming to rest on Henry. 'I'll leave you in command, Henry,' he said quietly, and as the older man nodded in reply he added, 'I think it might be a good idea if everyone were to get back inside the plane until we return.'

Amid a ripple of speculation, they returned to the sanctuary of the plane while Jack and William prepared to venture into the bush.

At last they were ready, but it was with a sense of trepidation that Toni watched them go.

'Take care,' she called out on a sudden impulse.

Jack looked over his shoulder and briefly his gaze met hers then he lifted his hand in reply.

'We will,' he answered.

Then they were gone, swallowed up by the fierce thorn thickets.

As she turned back into the interior of the plane

Toni felt a sense of desolation creep over her—an overwhelming feeling of loss. What if Jack didn't return? What if anything should happen to him?

Desperately she tried to pull herself together. It wouldn't do to let the others see how she was feeling—it would only depress them.

But as she turned away she was suddenly conscious of someone watching her. Diaka was sitting on the floor of the plane, her knees apart but drawn up either side of her chest, her solemn, unblinking stare on Toni. In that instant Toni knew the African girl had read her thoughts.

It grew hotter and hotter in the plane.

The waiting seemed to go on forever. In reality it could have only been about forty minutes since Jack and William had gone, but to those who waited it seemed like eternity.

'What I can't understand,' said Ruth irritably as with her uninjured arm she fanned herself with a brochure advertising the delights of an African safari, 'is why no one has come looking for us.'

'They probably have,' said Henry with a sigh; 'they just don't know where to look.'

'If it hadn't been for those storms we wouldn't be in this mess,' complained Ruth. 'You'd have thought that pilot would have known it wasn't safe to fly, wouldn't you?' she added in disgust.

'It was safe,' said Hilary, poised to defend Lutas. 'It was hardly Lutas's fault that the storms circled back.'

'Huh!' Ruth sniffed and, using her brochure more ferociously, began to swat the interminable flies that swarmed around their heads, clustering around eyes and mouths.

'You'll get even hotter doing that,' observed Toni.

'God, I'm thirsty,' muttered Henry, mopping his face and neck. 'Isn't it time for rations again?'

'Afraid not.' Hilary pulled a face. 'But cheer up, we're going to open the other tin of soup later.'

'That's great, for today,' said Paul who was lying full-length across two seats, his hat over his face, 'but what do we do tomorrow. . .and the day after. . . when we don't have anything. . .?'

'Paul. . .' began Toni warningly, but there was no stopping him.

Removing his hat, he sat up and looked round at the others. 'I saw a film recently,' he went on relentlessly, 'where these people were in a plane crash. It was in the snow in some remote mountainous region. They lived on snow for a while but then, when they were on the point of starvation, they ate the bodies of their comrades who hadn't survived——'

'Paul!'

'Oh, my God!' moaned Ruth, flapping her brochure even more frantically.

'Toni. . .?' A choked cry from the far corner of the cabin suddenly diverted their attention.

Toni turned her head and to her dismay saw that Henry was slumped on the floor against one of the seats and was clutching his chest. His high colour of only moments earlier had gone, replaced by a greyish pallor. With a start she scrambled to her feet and moved rapidly across to him.

His breath was coming in short, sharp gasps. She

knelt beside him, attempting to lie him flat, then paused as he managed to whisper. 'Tri-Trinitrin. . . in. . .my luggage.'

Immediately she turned to Paul. 'Which is Henry's bag?' she demanded.

'That one.' He pointed to a green and grey striped holdall and Toni dragged it towards her, unzipped it and began rummaging inside. To her relief she quickly found the bottle marked glyceryl trinitrate and unscrewing the cap tipped one of the tiny white tablets into her hand.

Then, crawling back to Henry, she said urgently, 'Come on, Henry, open your mouth, let's get this under your tongue.'

He obeyed instinctively even though his eyes were closed and his nostrils white and pinched with pain.

'Is he all right?' Paul's face, also white and frightened, hovered over Toni's shoulder.

'He's having an angina attack,' said Toni briefly. 'I would imagine it isn't his first if he has prescribed medication.'

'But will he be all right?' persisted Paul.

'Hopefully, yes. Trinitrin acts fast. I just wish he'd warned us this might happen,' said Toni grimly.

'He probably didn't want to worry you,' said Paul.

Toni sat by Henry until the Trinitrin began to act, but even after that she could guess by the pallor beneath the two-day-old stubble on his jaw that he was still in considerable pain.

'Why didn't you say?' she asked at last when he opened his eyes and looked up at her.

'No one knew.' He gave a great sigh. 'If my company

had known, I don't think they would have let me make
this trip.'

'Was it so important?' she asked gently.

'Yes.' He managed a slight shrug. 'A lifelong
dream. . .I knew it was the only way I'd get to see
Africa. My wife. . .she doesn't like to travel. . .we
take our holidays in Cornwall each year. . .'

'Does she know about your angina?'

'Yes, but not how bad it is. . .' He trailed off and
closed his eyes again. 'She wouldn't have let me come
if she had.'

'Oh, Henry,' said Toni, then gently she smoothed
back the thinning strands of his hair

After a while he dozed and Toni glanced anxiously
at her watch. Jack and William had been gone for
nearly an hour and a half.

'Is he feeling better?' Hilary came and crouched by
her side.

'I think so—his pain has lessened,' whispered Toni.
'Are the others back?'

Hilary shook her head. 'No, not yet.'

'I hope they haven't get lost.'

'I'm glad Jack took William with him—he at least
is more familiar with the bush than anyone else.' Hilary
paused. 'Did you know that Lutas is awake?'

'No, I didn't.' Toni sat back on her heels and glanced
down the plane to the area behind the cockpit and saw
that Paul was talking to Lutas. 'I hope we don't run
out of morphine for him,' she said.

'Aren't there painkillers in the medical supplies?'
asked Hilary anxiously.

Toni shook her head. 'No, there were mostly

dressings; the only analgesics we have are what Jack was carrying in his bag.'

'The situation could get very grim, then,' Hilary lowered her voice so that none of the others could hear.

'It could,' agreed Tony. 'On the other hand we have been fortunate to be carrying what we were. God knows how we would have coped without any form of medication.'

The day dragged on and it grew even hotter; the interior of the plane, which had once been such a sanctuary, now began to resemble some sort of giant furnace, and as the minutes ticked by Toni found herself praying that Jack was safe and that he and William would return soon.

Just as she was beginning to give up hope, unable even to voice her fears to Hilary who she knew was having the same thoughts, a shout went up from Paul who was sitting in the open doorway.

'They're back!' he cried.

A murmur of relief rippled through the others, Toni stood up and moved rapidly to the doorway and was just in time to see Jack and William trail wearily through the thorn bushes into the clearing.

They both looked tired and dishevelled, their clothes torn where the wicked thorns had ripped at them, their shirts soaked with sweat.

Toni couldn't remember ever having been so pleased to see anyone in her entire life.

As the pair approached the plane Jack looked up, saw her watching him, tilted his hat to the back of his head, and in spite of his fatigue managed a smile. His face was grimy with dust while rivulets of sweat had trickled from beneath his hat and disappeared into the stubble on his jaw.

'Hi!' he said as his eyes met hers.

'Any luck?' she asked as he eased his way past her into the plane.

''Fraid not.' With a deep sigh he tossed his hat into a corner. 'We walked in an easterly direction but we couldn't see anything that even resembled a landmark—just miles and miles of unending bush. We backtracked in a circle,' he went on after a moment, then, glancing at the African, who had followed him into the plane and was crouching in a corner resting, he added, 'Thank God I had William with me—I would have been lost without him.'

William, hearing the remark, lifted his head and smiled. 'I just follow vultures,' he said. 'They're still up there.'

'Still waiting,' said Hilary with a touch of despair in her voice.

'Did you see any other wildlife?' asked Paul eagerly.

'A couple of buffalo,' replied Jack as he sank thankfully on to the floor, 'and once, in the distance, we saw a herd of zebra, which suggests we may not be too far away from water—the problem is finding it.' Wearily he drew his hand across his face then looked up. 'Did Henry get the radio going?'

'Er. . .no.' Toni shook her head and glanced down the plane to where Henry was resting.

Jack must have sensed her air of concern, for he frowned. 'Is there anything wrong?'

'Henry had an angina attack,' Toni replied briefly.

For a moment Jack simply stared at her, the questions unspoken, but reflected in his eyes.

'It's OK,' said Toni quietly. 'He had Trinitrin with him.'

'Why didn't he tell us?'

'Apparently he didn't tell anyone—he had the idea that if his company knew, it might jeopardise his chance to make this trip.'

With a deep sigh Jack rested his head in his hands.

Toni left him to rest and went outside with Hilary to help prepare their rations.

While they were distributing the soup and counting out biscuits Toni and Hilary were surprised to be joined by Diaka, who seemed to have risen from her state of lethargy and appeared keen to help.

Hilary gave her the rations for Lutas and Henry and the African girl disappeared inside the plane. The girls were joined by Paul, Ruth, William and Jack and a little later by Diaka. They sat in a patch of shade cast by the wing of the Dakota and began the solemn business of eating their main meal of the day and drinking their water ration.

'Let's pretend it's a feast,' said Paul desperately.

'We don't need to pretend,' replied Hilary. 'To some people this would be a feast.'

'True,' agreed Jack. 'I was in Somalia recently and believe me, what we have here would have been a feast to those poor souls.'

They ate in silence after that, savouring every drop of their minute helpings of the vegetable soup and taking care to collect every last crumb from the digestive biscuits. The water wasn't as fresh as it had been the day before, but to their parched throats it seemed like nectar from the gods.

When every drop and morsel was gone, Paul stood up and wandered a little distance away. They knew he was battling with hunger pains and no one called him back.

'Soon be dark again,' observed William, glancing at the sky.

'Yes.' Jack climbed reluctantly to his feet. 'Time to build up another fire.'

He stretched and as Toni watched him she found herself once again thanking God that he and William had returned safely.

It was at that moment that she realised Jack had stopped and was listening, his arms still raised above his head.

'What is it. . . Jack. . .?' she asked as William too lifted his head.

'Listen!' said Jack.

They all listened and there it was, the unmistakable sound of an aircraft's engine.

Before anyone could move, Paul suddenly erupted back into the clearing shouting and waving his arms.

'It's a helicopter! They've come! It's a helicopter!' he yelled.

CHAPTER NINE

EVERYONE moved at once, rushing forward into the clearing waving their arms and shouting to attract the attention of the occupants of the silver helicopter hovering above the bush, far to the North of the stricken Dakota.

'Oh, thank God,' cried Ruth, tears streaming down her face. 'I knew they'd come; my husband has great influence, you know.'

'I hope they've got food aboard,' yelled Paul, still jumping up and down and waving his arms in uncontrollable excitement.

Toni joined the others, relief flooding over her as the moment of rescue seemed imminent.

Afterwards, she wasn't sure at what point the state of euphoria changed, because it all happened so suddenly. One moment they were all shouting and waving; even Henry had stumbled to the doorway of the aircraft and was shouting a commentary of events to Lutas who was unable to see what was happening, and the next, the helicopter banked and veered away to the east and the mood had changed, the shouts of joy becoming filled with alarm.

'They're going away!'

'My God, they haven't seen us!'

'Come back! We're over here!'

Then gradually as the helicopter became a mere

123

speck in the sky the frenzy died down and the awful truth settled like a pall.

In the end Hilary broke the dreadful silence. 'Do you think they did see us and they've gone to get help?'

'I suppose there's always a chance. . .' Jack shrugged and turned away, his head bowed.

'Surely, if they had, they would have given us some indication—they must know how we would be feeling.' It was Paul who put into words what they were all thinking. 'No,' he added brutally. 'They didn't see us and that was that.'

'Maybe they weren't looking for us,' said Toni. 'Maybe they didn't even know about us.'

'Of course they knew,' cried Ruth. 'They must have been looking for us; what else would they have been doing?'

Toni shrugged helplessly, recognising the note of hysteria in Ruth's voice and knowing it was no good trying to reason with her.

'Besides,' the older women went on, 'they will come back. . .when they don't find us, they will come back. . .my husband will make sure of it.'

'They won't keep searching the same area. . .' began Paul.

'Of course they will!' Ruth's voice grew even more shrill. 'They will be back, I tell you.'

'Yes, but when?' muttered Paul. 'The rate it's going, we could all be dead from lack of water. . .and food,' he added desperately.

'Shut up, Paul,' said Jack firmly. 'Ruth, pull yourself together.' He glanced round at the others. 'We simply have to face facts. They didn't see us this time, so we've just got to get on with it until they come back.'

'I thought they would have spotted the plane.' Toni turned and looked at the Dakota.

'It must be more hidden from view than we thought,' said Jack. 'The only answer is to keep the fire going day and night; that way maybe the smoke will act as a signal.'

'But what will we burn?' asked Hilary anxiously. 'All the packing cases went last night.'

'Well,' Jack looked round, 'we're surrounded by thorn bushes, so we burn those. Come on Paul, William, let's get cracking and build up another fire.'

A sense of despair had gripped them, however, and it was with a decided lack of enthusiasm that they collected dead wood and branches and piled them in the clearing.

'How long will the water last, Hilary?' asked Toni in a low voice as the two of them dragged a large thorn branch that had been ripped off by the wing of the Dakota.

'Only until about noon tomorrow,' Hilary replied in the same low tone.

'I think the best we can hope for is that the helicopter crew actually did see us.' Toni stopped and, straightening up, wiped the sweat from her eyes. She was about to bend to pick up the branch again when a flash of blue caught her eye. She paused and peered into the bush.

'What is it?' Hilary's eyes widened in fear.

'I don't know,' whispered Toni, edging forward.

'Careful.' Hilary caught at her sleeve, pulling her back. 'It might be an animal.'

'If it is, it's wearing a blue coat,' muttered Toni, pulling away from Hilary and creeping even further forward.

Carefully, avoiding the vicious thorns, she parted branches and from a small, natural hollow in the ground Diaka's liquid black eyes gazed up at her.

The girl was sitting very still, her thin arms over her head, but one glance at her face was enough to tell Toni that the African girl had gone into labour.

She crouched in front of her and stretched out her hand, gently running the back of her fingers down the girl's cheek. 'Don't be afraid,' she said softly. 'We'll take care of you.'

Diaka's expression never changed but Toni had the feeling the girl knew what she had said. Glancing over her shoulder, she saw that Hilary was standing behind her, an anxious expression on her face.

'Would you get Jack please, Hilary?' she said quietly.

Without a word Hilary turned and hurried back into the clearing.

Toni sat close to Diaka and held her hands, murmuring encouragement as a contraction shook the girl's body.

Even as they sat there, the fiery glow of the sky deepened and the sudden African night descended, stealing across the bush like a soft velvet blanket, and by the time Hilary had found Jack and he'd hurried to the spot it had grown quite dark.

Calmly he crouched beside them and touched Diaka's arm. She lifted her head and softly he spoke to her in Swahili.

She answered him and he spoke again. Diaka then briefly rested her head in her hands.

'What did you say?' whispered Toni.

'I asked her to come back to the plane,' replied Jack.

'Doesn't she want to?'

'No, she prefers the privacy of the bush to give birth.'

'Can't we let her?'

'We could,' he replied, 'but you know how cold it was last night.'

Toni was silent for a moment, considering, then she touched Jack's arm and he turned his head. Just for one moment she saw the sharp line of his profile etched against the darkening sky.

'Suppose we persuade the others to stay in the plane; would Diaka move nearer to the fire then?'

'I'll ask her.' He turned and spoke again rapidly.

There was no reply from Diaka and Toni was just wondering how they would manage to deliver the child in such a confined space, when Diaka moved, and gracefully, rose to her feet. With her back straight, she walked slowly and with great dignity out of the bush towards the glow of the fire.

With a sigh of relief Toni scrambled to her feet and began to follow Jack, but in her haste, in the darkness, she tripped over the trailing roots of a thorn bush. She gave a sharp cry as several vicious thorns dug into her arm and leg. Then she felt Jack's hand beneath her elbow and he was helping her to her feet.

'Are you all right?' he murmured in her ear.

'Yes, oh, yes,' she replied, feeling foolish and glad of the darkness which hid her confusion.

He didn't release her immediately, however, and she

found herself stiffening, taut, wondering what he was
going to do as his hand tightened on her arm.

'It could be a long night, Toni,' he said quietly at last.

'Yes, I know. . .'

'Henry could still need attention. . .'

'I know. . .'

'Lutas is far from out of the wood. It may not be
straightforward for Diaka. . .'

'We'll cope somehow.'

'That's my girl.' He squeezed her arm again and
sudden ridiculous pleasure surged through her.

Together, side by side, they walked back to the clearing, then, as they approached the fire, Toni realised
Jack was chuckling.

'What is it?' She half turned to him in surprise.

'If you think that's the extent of our problems you
can think again.'

'Oh, God, what now?'

He stopped. 'You hear that noise?'

She too paused and listened as a raucous, manic
sound echoed in the stillness.

She half turned towards him, 'It's only hyena, isn't
it? That's what William said earlier on.'

'That's right, that's exactly what it is,' Jack agreed.

'Well, at least it's laughing,' she said cryptically.

'Ah, but when it laughs,' replied Jack, taking her
arm again, 'it means there are lion around.'

She shivered, then shrugged. 'Oh, well, what's one
more problem on top of all the others? Besides, didn't
I read somewhere that big cats don't like fire? If that's
the case, we'll be OK. By the looks of it, William is
trying to start a bush fire.'

Indeed as they reached the clearing, the flames from the camp fire were leaping high into the air casting dark, eerie shadows on the edges of the bush.

Diaka took herself to the edge of the shadows and squatted on the ground while Jack beckoned to the others and indicated for them to join him inside the plane.

Toni stayed near Diaka although the girl turned her back to her. The only indication that she was in labour were the contractions that racked her slight body every ten minutes or so.

Jack joined them after a while, carrying what appeared to be a pile of bush jackets and other clothes, his medical bag, and the large plastic water container.

'There isn't much left,' he said, tipping it sideways, and in the light from the fire surveying its contents, 'but the others were adamant that Diaka should have as much as she needs.'

Toni swallowed and suddenly found herself unable to speak.

'They also each contributed one item of clothing from their luggage so we have some material to help with cleaning up later on, and I've brought these jackets to help keep us warm.' Jack tossed the jackets to the ground.' I've given Henry more Trinitrin,' he went on, 'and Lutas has had another injection—there's only one left, by the way.'

'Everyone else all right?'

'I think so. . .except for young Paul. . .'

'What do you mean?' Toni frowned and looked up. Paul had been fine less than an hour ago. 'What's wrong with him?'

'I'm not sure; he seemed to be acting a bit strangely. . .I hope he's not heading for an asthma attack.'

'Maybe it's just hunger,' said Toni hopefully.

'Yes, maybe.' Jack nodded. 'How are you coping with hunger pangs?'

'I try and think about something else.' She paused. 'What about you?'

'I'm starving,' he admitted. 'But I keep telling myself humans can survive several days without food. It's water that's essential.'

'And we don't have too much of that.' Toni shifted her gaze to the almost empty container.

Jack walked across the clearing and crouched beside Diaka. Toni heard him talking quietly in Swahili and the girl's muttered responses. After a few moments he returned and sat on the ground by her side.

'She wants to stay where she is. I tried to get her to agree to an examination. She's very reluctant but I expect she'll think about it.'

'Would she let me do it?' Toni glanced across at the girl's outline just visible in the shadows.

'That's what I'm counting on,' he replied, 'I'm hoping for a straightforward, normal delivery. Diaka is young and healthy, but we mustn't forget the traumas she's been through lately—she was attacked and raped and I can't imagine her diet has been too impressive in the last few months. I'm pretty certain of one thing, however, and that is that she won't let me anywhere near her.'

'I would have thought she had got used to having you around in Jabhati.'

'Maybe she did,' Jack replied wryly, 'but childbirth is another matter—that's definitely women's work.'

'It's a good job I'm here, then, isn't it?' she said lightly.

She didn't expect an answer and was surprised when he said, 'Yes, Toni, it is a good job you are here.'

Something in his tone made her pulse race faster and to cover her sudden confusion she glanced at Diaka and said, 'Shall I try to examine her now?'

'No,' he sighed, 'leave her be, for a while at least. She will want to be alone in these early stages. Later, well, later——' he gave a slight shrug '—it may be a different story.'

'I hope it isn't a breech birth,' she said after a moment.

'I'm sure you'll cope, Dr Nash,' he replied, and in spite of the darkness that hid his expression she detected a note of amusement in his voice. 'Didn't you say you'd just done a spell on Maternity?'

She threw him a quick glance but he had drawn his knees up and was resting his head on them as if weariness had finally overtaken him.

'I did, but conditions here are a far cry from what I've been used to.'

'That's what I've been trying to tell you all along,' he said gently. 'Out here it's all a far cry from what we've been used to.' He paused. 'Improvisation,' he went on after a moment, 'that's the name of the game in the bush, whether it's at the station in Jabhati or out here in the wild. Making do with what we've got and going without what we haven't. It's all as far removed from your shiny British hospital with its up-to-date equipment and modern technology as it's possible to be.'

She remained still for a long while watching the flickering of the flames. Gradually the voices from inside the aircraft grew silent and the only other sounds to be heard were the distant, manic laughter of the hyena and the intermittent call of some night bird summoning its mate.

She grew warm and drowsy and must have dozed for a while, and in the end it was another, recurring sound that roused her.

At first she thought it was an animal, for it was a low, unusual, mewling sound. She lifted her head to listen and in that instant she realised the sound was coming from the shadows beyond the fire.

Soundlessly she got to her feet and, pausing only to pick up Jack's medical bag from the ground and the pile of clothing, she moved lightly across the clearing towards Diaka.

As she approached, the girl lifted her head and in the firelight Toni saw the glitter of fear in the large, dark eyes. It was she who was making the mewling noises, uncanny sounds that started as a growl deep in her throat then rose to a high-pitched sound that seemed to hang in the darkness.

'It's all right, Diaka,' she said softly noting that the girl was sitting in a pool of water. 'I'm here. Lie down and let me see what's happening.'

Somehow the language barrier ceased to be a problem and instinctively Diaka did as Toni told her, lying on the ground while Toni took a stethoscope from Jack's bag.

The baby's heartbeat was loud and strong and with a smile Toni gave the universal thumbs-up sign to Diaka. Then in the light from the fire Toni examined her, finding to her surprise that the girl's cervix was already well dilated.

Quickly she arranged some of the jackets on the ground a little closer to the fire, then somehow she persuaded the girl to move.

She had no sooner got Diaka settled more comfortably on the clothing than another contraction racked her body. Toni gripped her hands as the inevitable but uncontrollable urge to push overpowered Diaka.

As she held her, offering support and encouragement, indicating how she should breathe, another sound filled the vast African night, a loud, awesome, roaring sound.

Lion, thought Toni absent-mindedly, lifting her head for a fraction of a second to listen. Jack had been right about the hyena's laughter.

Then Diaka grunted again and she forgot everything as the girl prepared to give birth.

Once, Toni glanced across the clearing and saw that Jack was no longer asleep by the fire. Instinctively she knew he was behind her in the shadows offering silent support, being there if she should need him.

With two more massive contractions the baby's head was born.

Firmly Toni held the head, feeling beneath her fingers the soft fuzz of dark hair, at the same time trying to demonstrate to Diaka to take short, sharp, gasps of breath to slow down the birth.

Moments later with a further contraction the little body slipped into the world.

Toni looked at Diaka and, seeing the question in her eyes and knowing she couldn't understand, she lifted the tiny baby so that in the firelight Diaka could see her daughter.

With a length of bandage Toni firmly tied the cord then cut it using a scalpel blade from Jack's bag. She then wrapped the baby in a cardigan, a cardigan so soft it felt like cashmere and which could only belong to Ruth, and without further preamble placed it in its mother's arms, covering them both with a large bush jacket.

Only then did she pause for a moment to sit back on her heels and with her heart bursting briefly shared Diaka's joy.

Something made her turn. Jack was standing behind her, he too watching the scene.

She scrambled to her feet, turned and literally fell into his outstretched arms.

For a timeless moment he held her close, so close she could hear the steady beating of his heart.

'Well done,' he whispered softly against her hair.

For a few seconds she was content to remain there, leaning against him. In fact, she thought, really, she would be perfectly happy to remain there for ever in the safety of his arms.

Then gradually she became aware of rustlings, murmurings behind them in the darkness. She stiffened, her eyes widening then realised that Jack didn't seem in any way perturbed.

'What is it. . .?' The question died on her lips as he

gave a soft chuckle and held her even closer.

'It's the others,' he said briefly.

'Really. . .?' She turned in surprise; she'd imagined everyone else was asleep.

'I suppose we'd better put them out of their misery.'

Just before he turned away she felt the fleeting brush of his lips against her cheek, a kiss so soft that afterwards she wondered if she'd imagined it.

'It's a girl!' he called, his voice echoing around the clearing, hitting the rock face and bouncing back.

Immediately a loud cheer went up from deep in the shadows between the fire and the Dakota, and in that instant Toni realised the others had been sitting there in the darkness, waiting for news.

The next hour was spent in a flurry of activity as Toni turned her attentions to Diaka and her baby once more. One further contraction produced the placenta, which Jack took away to inspect then dispose of.

Toni lifted a beaker of water to Diaka's lips, and as the girl drank deeply and gratefully she was pleased to see that the baby was already suckling at the breast.

Just as the sky began to lighten with the first touch of dawn they managed to persuade Diaka to return to the aircraft to rest.

With her baby still nestling close, and declining all but the lightest offers of assistance from Jack, the African girl walked gracefully across the clearing, her head high, her back straight, defying all evidence that she had just given birth.

'You too should get some rest,' said Jack to Toni. 'It's been quite a night.' He grinned. 'Even the lions' serenade seemed part of the occasion.'

'I hardly noticed it.' Toni laughed weakly. 'Any other time I would have been terrified that they were about to attack. . .but as it was. . .' She shrugged and trailed off, then, throwing him a glance, she said, 'I'm not the only one who needs rest. . .you do too, Jack.'

'I might just take your advice,' he nodded, 'and get my head down for a couple of hours. No doubt the morning will bring its own crop of problems. . .'

'You can count on it. . .' She yawned, then, climbing wearily into the aircraft, stumbled down the aisle, briefly acknowledging words of praise from the others. Then, lying across two seats, she promptly fell into a deep, dreamless, sleep.

When she awoke, bright sunlight flooded the interior of the plane. For a moment she couldn't think what had happened, then she lifted her head and looked to the rear of the plane.

Diaka was lying on another of the seats, her baby on her breast. They were both asleep. She couldn't see Lutas from where she was lying but she assumed he was in his usual place. There was neither sight nor sound of any of the others.

She stretched, allowing herself the luxury of lying still for a few more minutes. Her mouth felt unbearably dry, her throat rough and parched, and the inevitable hunger pangs gnawed at her insides like some living monster, but in spite of her discomfort she was aware of a deep sense of pleasure, an excitement that glowed inside her.

Was it simply because of Diaka's baby? She was thrilled by the safe, normal delivery, of course she was, but it wasn't only that. Her own personal pleasure had more to do with the warmth that was growing between herself and Jack—the sharing of responsibility that had brought them closer and closer together—the sharing of Diaka's joy—that wonderful moment when he had held her and his lips had brushed her cheek. Surely she hadn't imagined it? Surely it hadn't just been part of the magic of the African night? She stirred again and hugged herself, cherishing the memories.

She was shaken from her reverie by shouts from outside. Reluctantly she opened her eyes, then, as the shouts grew louder and more angry, she sighed and sat up, swinging her legs to the floor and groaning at the stiffness of her limbs.

Rubbing the sleep from her eyes, she made her way to the open doorway of the plane then paused, squinting in the bright morning sunlight as she saw the others grouped around the still smoking fire. They appeared to be arguing. They looked up as she appeared and fell silent.

'What is it?' Blankly she looked from one to the other, her gaze finally, inevitably, coming to rest on Jack.

'It's William,' he said shortly, meeting her stare.

'William?' She blinked stupidly. The tall African had until then been the very least of their problems. 'What's wrong with him?'

'He's gone,' said Henry.

'What do you mean, he's gone?' Wildly she looked

round, thinking for one moment they meant he was dead. 'Where's he gone?'

'You tell us,' muttered Paul. 'He's done a bunk in the night.'

CHAPTER TEN

'WHAT?' Toni stared from one to the other in bewilderment.

'Not only has he done a bunk,' snapped Ruth, 'he's taken our water container with him. It's absolutely typical. I said that one was going to be trouble right from the start—didn't I, Henry?' she demanded. 'Didn't I say that?'

'Yes, Ruth,' Henry admitted wearily. 'Yes, you did say that.'

'Trouble? What on earth do you mean, trouble?' Indignantly Toni glared at Ruth. 'William has been the one person who hasn't been trouble!'

'Looks as if he's made up for it now,' Ruth sniffed. 'God knows how long he thinks we'll survive without any water at all.'

'There was very little left in the container. . .' began Henry uncomfortably as if he was reluctant to believe the worst of William.

'Even so.' Ruth was not to be swayed, but at that moment a shout went up from Hilary who had suddenly disappeared back inside the plane.

'It's all right,' she called as she reappeared in the doorway, 'William may have taken the container, but he's left the water—a measure in everyone's drinking cup.'

A sigh of relief ran through the group and even

Ruth had the grace to look shamefaced.

'Where do you think he's gone?' Toni glanced uneasily at Jack, noticing how tired and drawn he looked.

'Who knows?' Jack shrugged. 'Your guess is as good as mine. . .'

'So what would your guess be, Jack?' It was Henry who posed the question, but everyone waited to hear the reply.

'I would like to think he's gone to look for water.'

'Do you think he'll find any?' Paul, who had been sitting close to the dying embers of the fire, looked up hopefully. He looked a bit flushed, but to Toni's relief he didn't appear to be wheezing.

'We can only hope,' replied Jack grimly. 'There certainly wasn't any sign of water when we went out before, but maybe he's gone in a different direction this time.'

'Has he taken the gun?' asked Hilary suddenly.

'No,' Jack shook his head. 'I have the gun.'

Hilary's eyes widened. 'What if he gets attacked? Those lions sounded really close last night.'

'They were further away than you think,' said Jack calmly, 'and besides, I should imagine William is well used to taking care of himself in the bush.'

'Maybe we should have sent him for help in the first place,' mused Henry.

'Maybe we should, who knows? But I would hazard a guess that we are too far in the wild for anyone to reach civilisation on foot,' replied Jack.

Silence greeted his words and it was the silence of despair, then in a determined gesture Jack pulled his

hat forward over his eyes and turned briskly to Toni.
'How's Diaka?'

'Sleeping,' she replied then added, 'and the baby.'

'Good. See that she is comfortable and has a drink.
We must change Lutas's dressings. Hilary, what food
is left?'

'Only biscuits,' she replied quietly.

'Right, share them out—don't forget Diaka,' he
replied abruptly then, turning to Henry and Paul, he
said, 'This fire must be built up—next time they come
looking for us, I'm going to make damn sure they
see us.'

With a sigh Henry turned away and Paul slowly and
reluctantly climbed to his feet.

'You OK, Paul?' Toni paused before going back to
the aircraft.

'Yeah, fine,' he mumbled.

'Breathing all right?'

He nodded. 'Hunger and thirst must keep asthma
at bay—I'll bear it in mind in future.' He gave a short
laugh but the cynicism of his joke somehow summed
up the hopelessness of their situation.

Slowly and with very little enthusiasm they went
about their tasks. Lutas seemed very weak that morning and was semi-delirious while Toni changed his
dressings. Jack gave him the final shot of morphine
then he and Toni left the pilot to rest and moved down
the plane to see Diaka.

The African girl looked up and smiled and Toni saw
that the baby was suckling again. While Jack examined
the baby Toni began tearing up some garments to use
as padding for both Diaka and the child.

'She's fine.' Jack lifted the baby up into his arms and stood for a moment smiling tenderly down at her. 'A beautiful baby,' he added, then said something in Swahili which Toni guessed had the same meaning, before handing the baby back to her mother.

When they'd finished with Lutas and Diaka and Jack had made sure that Henry had no further chest pain, Hilary shared out the few remaining rations and the last of the water.

They sat outside the plane as far away from the fire as possible to avoid the heat and tried to make their rations last as long as they could, all mindful of the fact that it could be the last morsels that would pass their lips for a very long time, if at all.

As the sun rose higher in the heavens a state of lethargy descended, the only activity being the swatting of the eternal flies that still swarmed around their heads and clustered around eyes and mouths.

'I shall never moan about English flies again,' muttered Toni. 'They seem tame and inoffensive compared to these. The only blessing is there don't seem to be the mosquitoes that there were in Nairobi.'

'True,' agreed Hilary sleepily, 'and have you noticed those damn vultures have stopped circling?'

'I hadn't.' Toni lifted her head to look. 'But you're quite right, they aren't around today. Maybe they've given up.'

'Don't you believe it,' said Paul darkly from the other side of the clearing, 'they're in hiding somewhere just waiting for one of us to kick the bucket, then they'll swoop down and start tearing flesh and picking bones. . .'

'Will you please keep your objectionable prophecies to youself?' said Ruth, but even her voice was subdued now, stripped of its acidity.

Toni glanced across at her, wondering how the older woman was really bearing up. She had ceased to complain about the pain of her shoulder, in fact she had ceased to complain about anything and had grown quite quiet. She had scraped her hair unattractively back behind her ears, her face was streaked with grime and dust and her cotton blouse was soaked with sweat, but it was the expression in her eyes that concerned Toni the most, for it was dull and lifeless. How much longer could she cope with these conditions? How much longer could any of them cope? A sudden shaft of panic shot through her and instinctively she transferred her gaze to Jack.

He was watching her. He was sitting on the ground a little distance from the others, his back against a tree. His hat was pulled well down over his eyes, but he was watching her from beneath the brim.

She was about to look away but he raised his hand, the gesture barely discernible, and motioned for her to join him.

Quietly, so as not to disturb the others, she got up and moved across to join him, dropping to the ground beside him, sharing the shade from his tree, resting her back against its trunk.

Neither of them spoke and when a little later she felt him cover her hand with one of his she made no attempt to remove it, content to let it remain, drawing comfort from his nearness.

Perhaps they would die like this, side by side—the

thought was terrible yet held a certain perverse allure, for at that moment in the sweltering heat of the day, in the grip of a thirst previously unimaginable, and with hunger eating at her insides, Toni felt she would be prepared to lie beside this man and quietly slip into oblivion. . .

On the other hand, it might be rather nice if he were to make love to her first. . . She felt a smile touch her lips at the thought. Was she starting to hallucinate? What the hell? What if she was? What would it be like, Jack Christy's lovemaking? Would it be passionate and masterful? Or would there be tenderness, the tenderness she'd seen in his eyes when he'd held Diaka's baby?

In spite of the intense heat, she shivered, then she gave herself a little shake. What in the world was she thinking of? Jack Christy wouldn't make love to her; he already had a woman—Shakira—whom he was probably thinking about at this very moment, thinking about, and longing for, wondering if he would ever see her again, hold her, love her. No, he wouldn't be interested in making love to her, Toni—it would be wrong. . .but then again, if they were going to die anyway, would it matter. . .?

The illogical thoughts chased each other round and round in her brain as the heat overcame her and with her hand still in Jack's she became drowsy and finally slept.

She awoke suddenly, jerked awake by the pounding of running footsteps through the dusty pathways between the thorn bushes.

She sat up quickly and was just in time to see William

run into the clearing. He was carrying the plastic water container in both hands. Jack was already on his feet, the others emerging more slowly from their heat-induced stupor.

William was breathless but beaming, a dazzling smile splitting his face from ear to ear as he held the container aloft for them all to see the water inside.

'Well, I'll be blowed, you old son of a gun!' Henry slapped him on the back. 'Where in hell did you find that?'

'Waterhole.' Gasping for breath, William handed the container to Jack then bent forward, his hands on his knees as he fought to regain his breath.

'Where?' Jack grasped the container and, holding it up, studied the contents.

William pointed in the direction of the rockface. 'The other side—there's a path through the rock—we went in the wrong direction before.' As he regained his breath he straightened up. 'It was lions last night, made me think water close, then at first light—vultures not there—they picking lions' kill.'

'You mean they weren't interested in us after all!' Hilary gave a short laugh. 'And there was me having nightmares about them. . . So how far away is this waterhole, William?'

'Two,' he shrugged, 'three kilometers, no more.'

'Well at least we won't have to ration water anymore,' said Paul, 'I'll get my cup,' he added.

'Hold on a minute,' said Hilary sharply and they all stopped and looked at her. 'The water will have to be boiled before any of us drink it.'

Paul stared at her in exasperation. 'Oh, come on,

Hilary, we all know you are a water expert but this is an emergency situation, for God's sake. We'll all die from dehydration soon. . .'

'I know,' replied Hilary sharply. 'I know only too well; I've had a gippy tummy for the last twenty-four hours—I was about to take up permanent residence in the latrine so I know all about dehydration——'

'You never said.' Toni stared at her in consternation.

'You had enough to get on with without me whinging,' replied Hilary tartly, 'but I'm warning you now, dehydration or not, if you drink that water as it is, you'll be asking for trouble.'

'Hilary's right,' said Jack firmly.

'So does that mean that poor William's gone to all this trouble for nothing?' asked Ruth indignantly, her earlier suspicions of William's intentions apparently forgotten.

'Not at all,' replied Jack.

'But Hilary said it would have to be boiled,' protested Ruth.

'Then we boil it.'

'But how. . .we don't have anything to boil it in. . .' Wildly Ruth looked round, but already Henry had walked away and was examining the torn wing of the Dakota.

Jack walked across the clearing to join him and Toni heard him say, 'Are you thinking what I'm thinking, Henry?'

Moments later Jack was hacking at the wing with Lutas's axe and within the hour the men had pulled a large piece of metal from the wing and had knocked it into a shape concave enough to hold fluid.

While they built up the fire to boil the precious water Jack suggested William take him to the waterhole.

'If there's water, there must be food,' he said simply, and William nodded.

They returned within the hour each carrying a dead bird.

'Some sort of guinea fowl,' Jack explained as they tossed the birds on to the ground. 'William caught them. They won't exactly make a feast between nine of us but they'll help to stave off the hunger pangs. . .'

'But how did he. . .?' began Paul anxiously, his hunger momentarily forgotten in his brief concern for the unfortunate birds.

'Don't ask,' replied Jack obliquely.

'It's probably best we don't know,' said Hilary. 'Besides, it's survival—the law of the wild.'

Paul nodded, his hunger overcoming his reserve.

The next hour was a frenzy of activity as nightfall fast approached. The fire was built high with thorn branches hacked down with the ever-obliging axe, the fowl were stripped, plucked and skewered on to make-shift spits where they were turned slowly over the fire, roasted to a turn, the mouthwatering aroma wafting across the bush.

The clearing took on a party atmosphere as they sat round the fire telling stories and cracking jokes. Every morsel was devoured with relish, every finger licked clean.

Afterwards, the bones were boiled in the remains of the water to make a soup for Lutas who was still semi-delirious, and for extra nourishment for Diaka to enable her to breastfeed her baby.

Still they sat on round the fire as if reluctant to break the spell of optimism that had reigned since William's discovery of the waterhole.

Henry began to talk of his daughter's forthcoming wedding, Hilary spoke of the promotion she was hoping for in her job and Ruth began to make plans to visit the grandchild in Canada whom she'd never seen.

'What about you, Jack?' asked Henry suddenly.

'Me?' Jack looked up, the sharp contours of his face softened by the firelight. 'What about me?'

'What plans do you have for the future?'

Suddenly Toni found herself holding her breath as she waited for his reply.

'You mean the future as it was before the crash or the future it may now have become?' asked Jack enigmatically.

'I don't know,' replied Henry after a moment's thought. 'You think there's a difference?'

'I don't doubt it,' said Jack quietly, picking up a stick and drawing patterns in the dust before him. 'I would go so far as to say that none of us will be the person he or she was before this experience. If we survive I would imagine our whole concept of life and what it's all about will have changed forever. I would also think it will have changed what we want out of life as opposed to what we thought we wanted.'

Silence greeted his words as if each of them were assessing their own dreams and ambitions, and Toni found herself wondering if Jack had meant he would now stop dallying and marry Shakira as soon as he could. The thought plunged her into misery.

'You think we will survive now, Jack?' asked Hilary.

'I think there's a much greater chance now we have water—we can certainly go for much longer and I can't believe the rescue services will abandon their search until they find us—it can only be a matter of time now.'

Suddenly, perversely Toni found herself hoping it wouldn't be too soon.

Then she gave herself a little shake. What in the world was the matter with her? Of course she wanted to be rescued—she'd been every bit as devastated as the others when the helicopter hadn't seen them. . .

But things had changed since then. . .they had proved they could survive in the wild. William had found water for them. . .and food. . .while she and Jack. . .she and Jack. . .

Abruptly she dismissed the thought even before it formed fully in her mind, and, climbing to her feet and wiping her hands down the side of her trousers, she walked away from the fire towards the aircraft.

She slept reasonably well that night, only stirring when Diaka's baby cried to be fed.

The next time she awoke was when someone touched her shoulder. It was still fairly dark and she could only just make out the shape of a figure bending over her.

'What is it. . .?' she began, then was silenced as the person touched her mouth with a hand, then when she was fully awake motioned her to follow.

It wasn't until she reached the doorway and in the glow from the fire saw it was Jack who had awakened her.

He jumped from the plane then turned to assist her, steadying her with one hand beneath her elbow.

'Is there something wrong?' she whispered.

'For once, no,' he murmured. 'I want to show you something.'

William was guarding the fire. He raised his head as they passed, then lifted a reassuring hand to Jack as if something between them had been prearranged.

Mystified, but trusting, Toni followed him unquestioningly into the darkness of the bush.

The vast African sky was still studded with stars but, even as they walked, the darkness began to fade and the opalescent glow of dawn lightened the bush. A soft mist hung on the tops of the thorn trees, its tendrils trailing like vines from the branches.

The path through the rockface was almost invisible, its entrance beneath thick undergrowth, but they found it in spite of the thorns which tore at their clothes and scratched their skin.

Like a tunnel the path ran for hundreds of yards through the rock, the sheer face soaring on either side, then, on emerging, more bush stretching as far as the eye could see, ghostly shapes against the lightening sky.

Just when Toni was beginning to wonder how much further Jack was taking her, fearing they would get lost, he stopped and, turning, took her hand, motioning with a finger to his lips for her to keep silent.

Drawing her forward, he began to climb a rise in the ground, and as they reached the top Jack dropped to his knees, motioned for her to do the same, then, parting a tangle of undergrowth, took her hand again and in silence indicated something before them at the foot of the incline.

The sight which met her eyes brought an involuntary gasp to Toni's lips. Before them stretched the waterhole, its surface smooth, its shores sandy.

In the foreground two water buffalo wallowed knee-deep, and gazelle and impala bent their graceful necks to drink, but it was the activity on the far side of the waterhole that ultimately caught Toni's attention.

A small herd of elephant had just arrived, their huge shapes eerie in the pearly half-light: a large bull, several cows, a few youngsters and two babies—perfect miniature replicas of the adults.

Even as she and Jack watched, several of the herd lowered their heads, great ears flapping as they filled their trunks, some to drink, others to play, squirting the water high into the air on to their own backs or the backs of their comrades.

'This was the Africa I wanted you to see,' whispered Jack. 'What you've seen so far has been pretty grim, but this is the magic.'

The scene became one of pure enchantment as the sun, like a ball of fire, quite suddenly rose from behind a distant belt of acacia trees bathing both waterhole and animals in its bright orange glow.

'Did you know there were elephant here?' whispered Toni.

Jack nodded. 'William and I saw their tracks that first time we went out. We agreed not to say anything.'

'Why? We knew there were lion about.'

'True,' he murmured, 'but a marauding lion could have been stopped with a bullet from Lutas's pistol; there would be no stopping a herd of stampeding elephant.'

'They look so gentle,' she whispered, watching enthralled as the members of the herd continued with their early-morning ablutions.

'I can assure you there wouldn't be much left of our camp if they decided they didn't like it.'

'Are there any lion around?' Nervously she glanced over her shoulder.

'You can bet on it. They'll be watching, awaiting their moment—the moment when one of those gazelle is off guard.'

Toni shivered slightly. 'You have the gun.'

He didn't answer and she looked up sharply then touched his arm in sudden alarm. 'Jack, you do have the gun with you?' she asked urgently.

'No,' he replied softly, 'I don't have the gun, I left it with William.'

Her eyes widened in sudden alarm. 'But what if. . .?'

'They won't,' he said firmly, then added, 'Not if we don't worry them, they won't. I couldn't take that risk with the others; they might panic.'

Something in his air of confidence and the way in which he trusted her reassured her, and she found herself relaxing again, watching the scene, fascinated once more by its beauty and simplicity.

In the end it was Jack who touched her arm. 'We must move,' he said softly.

'I could stay all day,' she murmured reluctantly.

'I know, but we must get back to the others. William will worry and come to look for us.'

Cautiously they stood up but the movement must have disturbed a flock of birds in the trees behind them, for they rose into the air with a great whirring of wings in a cloud of purple, yellow and red.

Toni gasped with shock and clutched at Jack and they stood transfixed, holding their breath as the elephants raised their heads and the gazelle turned then skittered away in fright.

But as the flock dispersed into the sky, calm returned to the scene, no tawny, feline shapes pounced from the bush and Toni let out her breath in a long sigh of relief and leaned weakly against Jack.

He held her, and they stood there together, she acutely aware of him; his nearness, the hawklike profile beneath the sweeping widow's peak of hair, the sinewy muscles under the khaki shirt, the deep tan from his years in the bush, and the steady stare from his grey eyes. Even the earthy male smell of him, accentuated by the harshness of their conditions, only increased the sense of excitement that was uncoiling deep inside her.

When he took her by the shoulders and gazed down into her face she was uncaring of the fact that her own hair was unkempt, that her skin was grimy, her shirt torn to tatters by the thorns.

He cupped her face, his hands hardened and scratched while she, in blissful oblivion, waited for his kiss.

Forgotten in that moment of piercing sweetness were all thoughts of Shakira and the fact that Jack was committed elsewhere, for, as his mouth closed over hers, all Toni was aware of was the warmth of the sun on her shoulders, the brightness of the dawn and her growing need for the man who held her.

She closed her eyes, shutting out his features, but as his kiss grew deeper, more probing, she felt his arms go round her, drawing her even closer, holding her against the taut hardness of his body. And to Toni it was familiar, so familiar, for it wasn't long since the last time he'd held her close. On that occasion he'd held her to warm her, all through that first night he'd held her, but it felt the same now, and she melted against him as if it were the most natural thing in the world.

Oblivious now to the beauty of the surroundings as the new day unfolded, they remained locked in their embrace until at last, reluctantly, Jack pulled away.

'I wish we could stay here forever,' he said shakily, gazing down at her.

'So do I.' She smiled up at him. 'Perhaps we should.'

'Don't tempt me.' A grim little smile quirked the corner of his mouth. 'If only it were that easy.' He paused. 'But we must go back, Toni.'

She stared at him. He meant back to civilisation. Away from this paradise, back to Shakira, back to real life. She swallowed and turned away. His kiss had meant nothing. How could it have done? It shouldn't have happened.

'They'll be sending out a search party from the camp at this rate.'

She paused. Was that all he had meant—back to the others?

He reached out and took her hand and her heart leapt.

For one wild moment she wondered if his kiss had meant something after all.

With one last look at the waterhole and its early morning visitors, they stole back into the bush and once again Toni was forced to remind herself that this man had a fiancée and that, if she allowed herself any delusions where he was concerned, she would surely be heading for certain heartbreak.

CHAPTER ELEVEN

HILARY met them on the edge of the clearing. She was clutching her stomach. She looked at each of them in turn and Toni had the sudden uncomfortable feeling that she knew exactly what had just taken place.

To cover her embarrassment, Toni said, 'Jack took me to see the waterhole—there were elephant drinking there. . .and other animals, it was quite beautiful, Hilary.'

'Yes, I daresay it was,' Hilary replied caustically. 'But I shouldn't let anyone bathe in it, Jack—one mouthful of that water could prove fatal.'

'You're right.' Jack replied. 'But we must let Paul see it—as far as he's concerned, it could almost compensate for the crash and make the whole thing worth while.'

'I doubt Paul will be too interested in anything at the moment.' Hilary bent almost double, hugging herself more tightly.

'Are you still getting the gripes?' Toni frowned.

Hilary nodded, pulling a face. 'Let's put it this way, if I'd eaten out, I'd be complaining to the restaurant.' She began to move away in the direction of the latrine.

'What's up with Paul?' Jack called after her. 'Is it his asthma?'

Hilary paused and looked back. 'I don't think so. But there's something wrong. You'd better have a look at him.' With that she scuttled away—all thoughts of being accompanied forgotten in her haste.

They moved on into the clearing and saw that William was boiling water in the metal container while Henry was chopping at yet more thorn bushes for fuel. He looked hot and uncomfortable.

'Take it easy, old chap,' shouted Jack. 'Don't overdo it.'

Henry paused, grunted and wiped his brow with the back of his arm then carried on hacking away with the axe.

They found Paul lying in a corner of the aircraft; his eyes were closed and sweat was trickling down his face. They crouched down on either side of him.

'Not feeling so good this morning, Paul?' asked Jack.

Without opening his eyes Paul shook his head.

'Is it your asthma?' asked Toni gently.

'No!' His eyes snapped open and Toni sat back on her heels, shocked by the vehemence of his reply.

'Steady on, old chap,' said Jack gently, 'Toni was only asking.'

'Sorry,' Paul muttered after a moment. 'It's just that everyone always assumes it's asthma with me.' He turned his head and closed his eyes.

'It's a pretty reasonable assumption, I would say.' Jack glanced at Toni.

She shook her head and frowned, indicating that she had no idea what could be troubling Paul.

'So are you going to tell us what is wrong?' Jack went on.

Paul remained silent.

'Do you have any pain anywhere?' Toni had

a go. 'Headache? Do you feel shivery?'

Still there was no reply.

'Maybe you just want to be left to rest.' As she spoke Toni reached out and patted his leg, Paul yelped in pain and jumped as if he'd been shot while in the seat behind him Diaka's baby set up a thin, wailing sound.

Jack had turned away but he swung back and stared down at Paul. 'What's wrong with your leg?'

'Nothing. . .there's nothing wrong with my leg,' gasped Paul.

'Well, if there's nothing wrong with it you won't mind us taking a look, will you?'

In a flash and without waiting for a reply Jack was on the floor of the plane beside Paul and had pushed the leg of his trouser up to his knee.

A piece of bloodstained material which looked as if it could have been torn from a shirt was tied round his leg. The flesh around the makeshift bandage was red and swollen.

'What the hell is this?' demanded Jack. 'When was this done?'

Still Paul didn't answer, but he gritted his teeth in pain as Jack began to unravel the bandage.

'When did you do it, Paul?' repeated Toni gently. 'Was it in the crash?'

Paul nodded and Toni watched fearfully, wondering what she was going to see, mindful of Lutas's terrible injuries.

When the wound was revealed, however, it did not appear too severe. It was only about two inches long and at first glance seemed no more than a bad scratch.

Toni gave a sigh of relief.

Jack, however, began to probe, and as Paul yelled out in pain pus began to ooze from the wound and Toni realised there was more wrong than she had at first thought.

'Why in God's name didn't you mention this at the time?' said Jack angrily. 'I specifically asked if there were any other injuries.'

'It didn't seem much,' muttered Paul.

'Didn't seem much! Surely even you must be aware how quickly things can turn nasty in these conditions.' With a muttered exclamation Jack stood up and looked at Toni.

'I'll get some water—you fetch a dressing pack and some antiseptic—that's all we can do.' As he crashed angrily out of the plane Toni looked down at Paul.

'Why didn't you say anything?' she asked curiously.

He sighed and closing his eyes again leaned his head back. 'All my life,' he said quietly at last, 'everywhere I've gone, I was always the one who had to be watched, the one who was expected to be ill. At games I wasn't ever allowed to do the same as the others, on school trips I was always a drag, always the one a teacher had to stay behind with while the rest went off and enjoyed themselves. Do you realise——' he opened his eyes and looked up at Toni '—this trip to Africa has been the first time in my life that my asthma hasn't affected me? Everyone was waiting for me to be ill, and I was so pleased not to be causing any trouble for once that when I discovered this——' he pointed to his leg '—I decided to keep quiet about it, hoping it would clear up on its own. Can't you understand that?' Pleadingly he looked up at her. He'd taken his glasses off and suddenly he looked very young, very vulnerable.

'Yes, Paul,' she replied quietly, 'I can understand how you must have felt—but you really should have told us, you know. Even if you didn't say anything at the time, you should have done so when it started to swell.'

'Yes, I suppose so,' he muttered grudgingly, watching her as she collected a dressing pack from the supplies and brought it back.

Jack reappeared at that moment with hot water in the second of the empty soup tins which he set down on the floor beside Paul. His anger seemed to have abated as he examined the wound again, then he cleansed it thoroughly with antiseptic solution which Toni added to the water.

'That's the best I can do,' he said at last, motioning for Toni to apply a dressing.

Afterwards, when they were well out of Paul's earshot, Jack voiced his fears. 'It's gone septic, of course, and it very much looks as if septicaemia is setting in.'

Hilary, who had returned from yet another trip to the latrine, was resting nearby and overheard Jack's remarks. 'Can you do anything for that?' she asked anxiously.

'We could if we had antibiotics,' he replied, and there was no disguising the frustration in his voice.

'And without?' Hilary threw a fearful glance towards the aircraft.

'Your guess is as good as ours.' It was Toni who answered her question.

'Jack!' A shout from the fireside made them turn. 'We need to think about food.' William, stripped to the waist, was banking the fire high. His dark torso glistened with sweat and his shoulders were bowed with fatigue.

Jack nodded wearily. 'What do you suggest?'

'If we took gun maybe we get antelope.'

As Hilary shuddered and turned away, Ruth stumbled from the aircraft and hurried towards them.

'I think you'd better come.' Her eyes darted wildly from Toni to Jack and back to Toni again.

'Is it Paul?' Toni began.

'No, Lutas—I think he's taken a turn for the worse,' muttered Ruth.

Without another word Toni followed Jack back into the aircraft and hurried to the little area they had managed to partition off for the injured pilot.

Mercifully he was unconscious so he no longer felt any pain. Jack examined him, then, as he checked his dressings, Toni caught a faint, sickly, but unmistakable smell.

She looked up sharply and her eyes met Jack's across the still form of the injured man. There was no need for words. The dreaded threat of gangrene hung in the air like some tangible thing.

Abruptly Jack stood up and indicated for Toni to follow him. As she scrambled to her feet however a wave of dizziness swept over her and she had to cling to the back of one of the seats until it had passed.

Jack must have realised she wasn't following him, for he stopped and looked back.

'What is it?' He looked anxious.

'Nothing—I just felt a bit faint, that's all—lack of food, I expect—I'm OK now.'

'Are you sure?' The tender concern was back on his face and she lowered her gaze.

'Yes—don't worry, I'm not going to fold up on you as well. I shall be fine when I've had one of William's antelope steaks,' she joked weakly, and as Jack turned away, seemingly unconvinced, she followed him outside.

'What should we do?' she asked in an attempt to change the subject. 'About Lutas, I mean.'

'Strickly speaking,' Jack began, then paused, hesitating while Toni waited, anticipating what was coming. 'I should amputate that shattered leg. . .' he went on at last, confirming her own fears.

'I would help all I could. . .'

'I know.' He paused again and looked down at her. 'Bless you for that,' he said, so softly that only she heard, 'but I'm not sure he would stand the shock. . . we have no morphine left and only a limited supply of local anaesthetic. . .'

'So what do we do?' In growing despair she stared at him.

He didn't answer immediately, appearing to consider, to weigh up the facts, then at last he seemed to reach a decision.

'Nothing for the moment,' he said firmly. 'We hope it doesn't spread. . .we amputate only as a very last resort. We also pray he remains unconscious,' he added grimly; 'he'll be in agony if he comes round. . .'

She felt sudden tears well up in her eyes. 'Oh, God, Jack,' she touched his arm, 'what are we going to do?'

'We stay calm,' he replied, taking her hands and gripping them tightly. 'At all costs, we stay calm. . .'

He stared into her eyes then he frowned, 'Are you sure you're all right, Toni? You've gone very white.'

'Yes, yes, I'm fine,' she muttered, but she felt far from fine. Her head ached and she still felt dizzy.

'Why don't you go and rest for a while?' Jack took her arm and steered her back towards the plane.

'I can't,' she protested. 'I have things to see to. . . Lutas. . . Paul.'

'Ruth can sit with Paul and I'll see to Lutas,' he replied firmly. 'No arguments, you get your head down for a couple of hours.'

She made no further protest, crawled to the little area of the plane she had made her own, curled up into a ball and thankfully closed her eyes, for the moment content to shut out the problems that threatened to be escalating right out of their control.

Her head still ached, and although she kept her eyes shut the light behind her closed lids seemed unbearably bright. This brightness slowly intensified until it exploded like a rocket in the sky on Guy Fawkes night, the thousands of coloured stars sinking slowly to earth.

Then there was blackness, cold, dark blackness where she shivered and shook, every bone in her body aching until unseen hands clawed at her and dragged her, screaming, back into the light.

There was peace in the lightness; she was in a garden—there were animals, leopards and cheetahs playing together with lambs and puppies, birds with beautiful plumage that rose *en masse* into a cloudless blue sky, the beating of their wings like some great orchestra.

There were voices too. Whisperings. Jack was there, but she could never quite reach him; she would stretch out her arms but always he remained just out of her grasp.

Hilary came too and tried to help her, whispered words of encouragement.

Once, when she managed to open her eyes, Diaka was there, bending over her, her great liquid eyes full of fear.

The darkness returned, only this time it was accompanied by heat, searing red heat as if she'd entered the very bowels of hell, and she fought and writhed as the demons threatened to possess her.

Someone was holding her, holding her close—she knew this place; she'd been there before, safe in these arms—a cup was held to her lips, cool water trickled into her parched throat, then ran out of the corners of her mouth when she could swallow no more, and ran down her neck.

Gentle hands sponged her face, smoothed her hair from her forehead just as her mother used to do then when she was a child.

There was swirling mist, then blackness again, but this time the blackness was free of devils, was soft, like black velvet; sweet, dreamless oblivion.

There were other voices; shouting, a roaring sound in her head that grew and grew until she feared her head would burst. Black shapes hovered over her, closing in—vultures come at last to claim their bounty.

She tried to scream but no one seemed to hear and she was lifted, lifted high until the warmth of the sun hit her face.

The roaring grew louder, the shapes larger, the voices more urgent.

In desperation she closed her eyes again, trying to shut out what would happen. Someone had said the vultures would tear flesh, pick bones. Who had said that? She couldn't remember. . .she must try. . .but she couldn't, it was impossible to concentrate. . .she kept drifting. . .

The roaring had become a steady drone. Somewhere close a baby was crying, a loud hungry cry. She was at work, in the maternity unit. . .the central heating was very noisy today. . .and why didn't someone feed that baby. . .?

Was this a cathedral, this high-roofed building, or was it heaven? That disembodied voice with the thick, Afrikaans accent. . .who could that be?

Yet more movement, screaming sirens, then white coats, green coats. . .once, blissfully, Jack's face close to her own; peace. . .then nothing.

She turned her head and opened her eyes. It was day-light but not so bright as she expected. Beyond the windowpane she could see the almost bare branches of a tree etched against a grey sky.

It was strange for the sky to be grey; it was always so blue or white in the heat of the day. . . She hadn't seen it this grey. And that tree. . .it didn't look like a thorn tree. . .it looked more like a horse chestnut with a few russet-brown leaves clinging to its branches.

She frowned and turned her head again, lifting it this time to look around. The effort caused her to wince, her neck ached and she felt incredibly weak.

She was in bed, in a small room. The washbasin, the striped cover, the curtains suggested a hospital but. . .

Any doubts were dispelled as the door opened and a nurse appeared, a black girl with a cheerful expression that broke into smiles when she saw that Toni was awake.

'Hello,' she grinned.

'Hello.' Toni managed a faint smile, tried to sit up then groaned.

'Gently does it—you've been pretty groggy, you know.' The nurse helped her into a sitting position and plumped up her pillows.

'What's been wrong with me?'

'I'm not really sure—Doctor will be along to see you soon.'

'Who found us?'

The nurse had been bustling around the room, but she paused and glanced at Toni. 'Found you? What do you mean?'

'We were in the bush. . .our plane crashed.'

'Oh, yes, I heard something about that,' the girl replied vaguely.

'So who rescued us?' Toni stared at her in bewilderment, wondering how she could be so vague over something so important.

'I'm sorry, I've only just come on duty. I've been on leave so I really don't know any details. You'll have to ask the doctor.'

'Doctor?' Her heart leapt. 'Dr Christy?'

The girl frowned. 'There's no one here of that name.'

'But he was with us. . .in the bush. . .'

'Oh, I see. So he doesn't work here?'

'No, he's with the VSO. He's stationed at Jabhati.'

'Where's that?'

'Jabhati. . .you must have heard of Jabhati.' Toni was beginning to have difficulty in controlling her impatience. 'It's in Tanzania.'

The girl laughed and shook her head. 'Sorry, but my geography isn't too good.'

'So where do you come from?' Exhausted with the effort of talking, Toni longed to close her eyes again, but there were so many questions she wanted to ask.

'Me? Oh, I come from Birmingham.' The girl straightened Toni's bedcovers. 'Would you like me to see if I can get you a cup of tea?'

'Birmingham? So how do you come to be working in Nairobi?'

The nurse had reached the door but she stopped and looked back at Toni, a mystified expression on her face. 'What do you mean, Nairobi? I've never been to Nairobi in my life.'

Toni stared at her. 'So where am I?' she whispered.

'What do you mean, where are you? You're in hospital.'

'I know, but where is this hospital? I thought it must be Nairobi. . .'

'Nairobi? You're in London!'

Weakly Toni leaned back against the pillows as with a laugh the girl disappeared through the door. But as if to confirm her words, and dispelling any further doubt that might linger in Toni's mind, a smattering of rain hit the windowpane.

CHAPTER TWELVE

LONDON? How long had she been in London, for heaven's sake?

And where were the others? What had happened to Lutas? And Paul? Were they here too?

And Jack—where was he?

She closed her eyes as the effort of thinking became too great, and felt tears seep from under her eyelids and trickle down her cheeks.

She must have slept then, for the next thing she knew the nurse was standing in the open doorway smiling at her.

'You have a visitor,' she said. 'Do you feel up to it?'

A visitor? Jack? Oh, please let it be Jack. She struggled to sit up, then fell back against the pillows.

The nurse must have seen her struggle as assent and stood aside for whoever was standing behind her to enter the room.

Dressed in a striped hospital dressing-gown and slippers, Hilary shuffled forward.

'Welcome back to the land of the living.' She grinned at Toni.

'Hilary!' Her eyes filled with tears again. 'Thank goodness you're here. I was beginning to wonder what on earth was happening.'

169

'You've been jolly ill.' Hilary sat down in the high-backed chair beside the bed.

'And you?' Toni stared at Hilary's attire.

'Oh, nothing too spectacular with me, just common or garden gastroenteritis—I'm going home later today—but you—well, Jack was worried about you.'

'Jack?' She looked up quickly, 'Is he here too?'

'No, he's still in Africa. . .'

Her heart sank. 'So why are we here? Who rescued us, Hilary? What happened?'

'Whoa, one question at a time!' Hilary laughed.

'Sorry, it's just that there are great gaps—I can't remember much.'

'An Air Rescue Service picked us up in the end—it was them who had been looking for us before, only that time they didn't see us. This time they saw the smoke from the fire. They took us back to a hospital in Nairobi.'

'The others? Was everyone all right?'

'The last I heard, Lutas was on his way to Theatre and Paul went straight into Intensive Care. Ruth and Henry were being checked over. I don't know what happened to William.'

'And Diaka?'

'Jack has taken her and the baby back to Jabhati.'

She stared at Hilary. 'So why are we here in London?'

'I asked to come back.'

'And me? Why am I here? I have a job to do.'

Hilary looked uncomfortable. 'It was on Jack's orders,' she said at last.

'What do you mean,' Toni demanded, 'on Jack's orders?'

'I'm sorry, Toni, I really don't know too many details, I was feeling pretty grotty myself at the time, but I did hear Jack talking to someone in the hospital in Nairobi and he was insisting that you be flown back to London. I was feeling so wretched I decided to come with you. Listen——' Hilary stood up '—is there anyone you'd like me to contact for you?'

'How long have we been here?'

'Four days.'

'Four days!'

Hilary nodded. 'As I said, you've been pretty ill. Jack feared malaria.'

'Malaria?' Her eyes widened. 'Surely not? I took my anti-malaria tablets religiously and besides, there weren't any mosquitoes in Tanzania.'

'Maybe not—but there were plenty in Nairobi. Remember all those on the airstrip?'

'I'd forgotten about those. . .'

'Don't worry, apparently your tests were negative. It was some awful nameless virus or fever—mind you, I'm not surprised—God knows what bacteria were in that water, even after boiling. It just proves how important WaterAid's work is, doesn't it?'

Hilary paused for breath, reflecting for a moment, then quickly carried on, 'Anyway, as I was saying, is there anyone you would like to see?'

She closed her eyes. Jack. She would like to see Jack. But Jack was in Africa. Jack had sent her back to England. Jack didn't want her in Africa. Jack had never wanted her in Africa.

'What about your mother, Toni?'

'My mother?'

'Yes, won't she be worrying?'

'She's away—she's in Australia visiting her sister.'

'Oh, I see,' Hilary frowned and tightened the cord of her dressing-gown. 'Well, is there anyone else?'

Wearily she shook her head. 'No, no one, Hilary. Thank you,' she added.

'Oh, well, in that case I'll go and get dressed. I'll come back and say goodbye before I go. I think they'll be keeping you here for a few more days, until you're really fit. . .' She paused, looking down at her, then quietly she said, 'What is it, Toni? What's wrong?'

'What do you mean, what's wrong?' She took a tissue from a box on the locker beside her bed and blew her nose. 'I'm ill, that's all.'

'No, it's more than that. You're unhappy—you're crying.'

She couldn't answer for the lump in her throat and the tears that threatened to choke her.

Hilary appeared to hesitate as if searching for the right words. 'It's Jack, isn't it?' she said softly at last, and Toni closed her eyes, unable to face the expression in Hilary's eyes.

'You're in love with him, aren't you?'

She knew she should deny it, knew her continuing silence only served to confirm it. She felt Hilary sit on the bed then take her hand.

'Do you want to tell me about it?' she asked softly.

Toni opened her eyes, and Hilary's sympathetic expression was almost her undoing.

'There's not a lot to tell.' She gulped. 'Nothing can come of it, as you well know.'

'I tried to warn you. . .'

'I know!' she exclaimed. 'I know you did, Hilary,' she added more gently, then with a helpless shrug she added, 'But I couldn't help it.'

'He really is a very attractive man—and a very unusual one,' admitted Hilary.

'He also belongs to someone else,' added Toni, trying hard to keep the bitterness from her tone.

'Ah, the lovely Shakira,' mused Hilary. 'I wonder how she would have shaped up in the same ordeal.'

'Goodness knows.' Toni shrugged again as if it were of little consequence.

'You know. . .' Hilary hesitated again. 'Jack was very impressed with the way you coped.'

'I find that hard to believe—don't forget he never wanted me there in the first place.'

'Even so, I think he was forced to eat his words— you more than proved your worth, Toni.'

'So much so that he packs me off home at the first opportunity. . .'

'Maybe he really was simply worried about you. . .' Hilary trailed off as Toni threw her a withering look.

'I think I just have to accept the fact that my mission to Jabhati is over.'

'You won't go back?'

She shook her head. 'Not there, no. I shall ask for another posting—Outer Mongolia or somewhere—as far away as possible.'

*　　*　　*　　*

How could she go back? Toni thought after Hilary had left. Even if he wanted her there, which was doubtful, how could she bear it, working alongside Jack, being near him twenty-four hours a day, possibly being there when he married Shakira? It would be more than she could take.

Hilary had been quite right when she had warned her that she really shouldn't have allowed herself to fall in love with Jack Christy—how could she have been so foolish?

And had she been that transparent? If Hilary had guessed the way she felt, had the others as well? And what of Jack himself—had he known? Had he encouraged her to love him? He had kissed her, after all. What of that? What of the time they'd spent watching the sun rise over the waterhole? Was that all it had been: Africa performing its magic? Had his attentions merely been circumstantial, his apparent concern for her no more than he would have shown anyone else?

It would seem so.

Miserably she turned her face to the wall. She would have to accept it.

And yet. . .and yet, a tiny thought persisted at the back of her mind. . .there had been something in his kiss, a passion that had shaken her—a tenderness that had surprised her. . .so much so that deep inside she knew she would never be able to forget him.

She grew stronger in the following days as her health gradually returned to normal. She telephoned her mother in Australia and put her mind at rest that not only was she safe but she was also well. News of the crash had apparently hit the headlines, and Toni knew her mother would have suffered untold agony waiting to hear if she was safe.

The medical staff at the hospital informed her that she was to have one further set of tests and, if they proved negative, she would be ready for discharge in a couple of days' time. They had also advised her that she should not consider returning to work for at least a month.

'A month?' She stared at the registrar in dismay. 'But why? I feel perfectly all right now.'

'You've been very ill,' he replied firmly. 'These tropical fevers are quite vicious and have been known to return—I advise complete rest for a while—a holiday somewhere quiet would be ideal.'

'How about a safari?' she attempted a feeble joke.

'Definitely not.' He didn't appear to have a sense of humour and peered sternly at her over his half-glasses.

She sighed. 'My cousin has a holiday cottage in North Wales. . .'

'That sounds far more sensible.'

'I'll give him a ring.'

She hadn't really wanted to come. North Wales in autumn could sometimes be grim, she knew that from the many holidays she'd spent here as a child. Her cousin's cottage was in the mountains just outside the village of Beddgelert near Snowdonia.

It was almost dusk when she arrived, but the caretaker who looked after the cottage had been forewarned and had turned on the heating.

She slept soundly that first night and awoke to pale

autumn sunshine that streamed through the bedroom window, lighting up the pink roses on the wallpaper.

When she had showered and dressed, she walked the mile or so into the village and bought milk, bread, a few other provisions and a newspaper. On her return to the cottage she lingered over a leisurely breakfast. The rest of the day she spent reading and walking, enjoying the spell of fine weather as she gradually felt her strength returning.

This was to set the pattern of her days at the cottage. She spoke to hardly anyone: there was no telephone and, apart from her daily trips into the village, she had no contact with the outside world.

She wrote to her mother, telling her something of what had happened, but as she relived the events on paper the memories, dulled by fever and drugs, came flooding back and at times were so painful that she was forced to put her pen down and walk away.

On the afternoon of the fourth day she went for a long walk, circling the village on one of the many mountain tracks and enjoying the peace of the spectacular Welsh scenery.

On her return she made herself a mug of tea which she took into the small conservatory at the rear of the building. Her cousin had only recently had the conservatory added to the property and it enabled occupants of the cottage to enjoy the view of the valley below, even when it was too cold to set foot outside the door.

It was warm in the sun and Toni leaned back in one of the two padded cane chairs, curled her hands round her mug and sipped her tea.

A dog was barking in the valley, the only sound apart from the low hum of an aircraft. Toni set her mug down on the tiled floor and closed her eyes.

How different the sun was from that fierce one in Africa. Hard to believe they were one and the same. The dog was still barking—howling really; it sounded like the hyenas. . .

The sun seemed to grow warmer, the light brighter, red and orange against her closed eyelids.

The hum of the aircraft sounded like lions roaring in the distance and surely that faint crackling sound was the camp fire?

If she opened her eyes, would she see William throwing thorn branches on to the fire, Henry hacking away with the axe. . .Diaka's smile as she fed her baby. . .? Would—oh, God!—would Jack be there? If she concentrated really hard, could she conjure them up—slip back in time. . .slip right back and relive that wonderful moment when Jack had held her in his arms?

She must have dozed, for in her dreams she was back; she was in the aircraft, but this time it was still in the air, Lutas at the controls and shouting for them to look out of the windows.

'Look!' he cried. 'Wildebeest—see them running! That's Africa—that, my friends, is what it's all about!'

When at last she awoke, it had grown cooler.

She lay still for a while, her eyes still closed, reluctant to break the spell, not wanting to return to the harsh truth of reality. The reality that it was all over, that they had all returned to their previous lives—had all picked up the pieces and were trying to forget.

She wasn't sure at what point she knew something was different, something had changed; she only knew it had.

She opened her eyes. The sun had almost sunk below the distant horizon and the valley was wreathed in a soft violet mist.

Slowly she turned her head.

Jack was sitting in the other cane chair, watching her.

Because she had been dreaming about him and her dreams had been so vivid, the shock wasn't as great as it might have been. In fact it seemed the most natural thing in the world for him to be there.

'Hi!' he said, his mouth quirking in the way she remembered so well.

'Hi!' she replied, then, as her senses gradually began to function, 'However did you find me?'

'With extreme difficulty.' He grimaced. 'Were you deliberately trying to hide?'

'Not particularly. They said I should rest. Get away from it all. I suggested a safari, but they didn't seem to think that was a good idea.'

'I'd say this is the next best thing.' He leaned forward as he spoke. 'Wonderful view.'

'Yes.' Her brain had suddenly come alive and shot into overdrive. Why had he come? What was he doing here? He was supposed to be in Jabhati. 'So how did you find me?'

'I tracked Hilary down in the end—she said you'd phoned her before you left, saying where you were going.' He paused. 'She didn't seem too sure about telling me at first,' he said at last.

'Didn't she?' Toni swallowed.

'No. In fact she gave me a dire warning about not upsetting you. Now why do you think she thought I might upset you, Toni?'

'I've no idea.' She tried to remain calm, but a quick glance at Jack's face revealed amusement in his grey eyes. Hurriedly she looked away.

'I told her I had no intention of upsetting you,' he added. 'I also told her I was concerned about you.'

'Why did you have me sent home?' she demanded.

'Because I thought you had malaria, because I wanted the best medical attention for you.' He frowned. 'Why do you think?'

'Because you didn't want me working for you,' she muttered.

'Oh, Toni.' He stared at her. 'You couldn't be further from the truth, believe me.'

'But you said that—at the beginning, you said that—you implied because I was a woman I would never cope.'

'I never questioned your professional expertise. . .'

'Maybe not. . .but you doubted my stamina. . .' She broke off and stared at him, then to her horror she felt her eyes fill with tears. 'And now,' she gulped, 'I've proved it, haven't I?'

'Proved what?' He shook his head.

'That I don't have the stamina necessary for Africa. I fold up at the first little bug that comes along. . .' angrily she brushed her tears away '. . .and that's another thing: all I seem to do is blub. . .'

'My dear girl.' He leaned forward and took her hands in his. 'That wasn't just a little bug, as you put it; it was a vicious virus with the power to kill. Coupled with that, you went through a very traumatic experience. . .'

'So did everyone else. . .'

'True, but you took more than your fair share of responsibility—you helped to keep morale up and you more than proved that you have stamina.'

'I did?' She raised her eyes to meet his, then was forced to look quickly away again as she found herself quite unable to cope with the expression she saw there.

'I still don't understand why you are here,' she muttered fiercely, trying to conceal her confusion. 'Hilary said you had gone back to Jabhati.'

'That's quite true, I did. I took Diaka home.'

At mention of the African girl Toni looked up, anxious for news. 'What happened? Her family? The baby?'

'They were so relieved she was safe that they welcomed her with open arms.'

'And the baby?'

'I suspect grandparents are much the same the world over,' he chuckled. 'The last I saw of them all, the baby's father was back on the scene and plans were being made for the future.'

'Well, that's a relief.'

'Talking of Diaka——' he paused and threw her a speculative glance '—there was just one other thing. . .'

'What's that?' She noticed his lips had curved into a smile.

'She's named her baby Antoinette—she wanted you to know.'

Toni flushed with pleasure.

'That's just about the greatest honour she could bestow. It's her way of saying thank you.'

'Well, it was one delivery I certainly will never forget.'

'I doubt any of us will ever forget any of it.' He sighed, growing serious again. 'Poor old Lutas certainly won't.'

'Lutas?' She looked up sharply. 'What's happened to him? The last I heard was that Hilary said he was in hospital in Nairobi about to go into Theatre.'

'He lost his left leg,' replied Jack quietly.

She stared at him in dismay. All their efforts with the brave pilot had been in vain.

Jack must have read her thoughts, for gently he said, 'He's alive, Toni.'

'I can't imagine a disabled Lutas.' Sadly she shook her head.

'Lutas being Lutas, he will cope,' replied Jack.

They were silent for a moment, their thoughts with Lutas, then Toni, suddenly remembering, said, 'And Paul, what about Paul?'

'As we thought: septicaemia.'

'Oh, God, no. Is he all right?'

'Yes, but only just, apparently. It was touch and go. They pumped him full of antibiotics. The last I heard he was making a slow recovery.'

'And the others? Ruth, William, Henry?'

'Ruth and Henry were flown home a few days ago. Ruth is to have physiotherapy on her shoulder. I phoned when I arrived in London, I gather she's already booked a flight to Canada——' he grinned '—travelling first class, I might add. Henry is to have his angina reassessed—it looks as if he may be in line for early retirement. William?' He paused. 'William flew on to Harare.'

'William was the only one to escape any trauma,' mused Toni reflectively.

'That's not strictly true,' Jack replied slowly.

'What do you mean?'

'When he reached Harare he found his mother had died. He was six hours too late.'

'Oh, Jack. How awful. Poor William. . .' She trailed off, in her mind's eye mental pictures of the tall, serious African with the wide, unexpected smile: tending the campfire, his bare back glistening in the glow from the flames; standing legs astride in the open doorway of the Dakota with Lutas in his arms; and running triumphantly into the clearing, the plastic drum of water held aloft.

After several moments of silence Toni looked at Jack again. He still held her hands but he had turned his head and appeared to be studying the view.

Slowly she withdrew one of her hands, lifted it and gently smoothed back his hair, revealing the red line of the cut against his hairline.

'It's healed nicely,' she said softly.

'Thanks to you,' he replied. 'There would have been a lumpy scar otherwise.'

'I see you've had the sutures out.'

He nodded.

'I was beginning to think maybe that was why you'd come to see me,' she smiled, 'so I could finish what I'd started.'

He remained silent for a moment then he glanced

up at her from under his brows.

'You're quite right,' he said at last, 'that is exactly why I came to find you—so that you could finish what you started. The only thing is, it has nothing to do with cuts or sutures.'

'Really?' She raised her eyebrows questioningly, but, as she waited for him to explain, her heart had started to do crazy things.

'I think, Toni, you know what I mean.'

'I do?'

'Let's not pretend.' He looked deeply into her eyes. 'During our time together, frightening and traumatic as it sometimes was, I gradually came to the conclusion that you cared for me.'

At his words her pulse began to race. But this was madness. Crazy talk. She remained silent, waiting for him to continue.

'What happened to us was a once-in-a-lifetime experience,' he went on quietly, 'but it taught me a lot of things about myself.'

'It did?' Her voice was barely more than a whisper.

He nodded. 'Was I wrong, Toni? Was I mistaken in thinking you might care?'

She stared at him. 'And what if I do care?' There was anguish in her voice now and she knew he must hear it. 'What could possibly come of it?'

'You mean you do?' Hope flared in his grey eyes.

Abruptly she snatched her hands away and stood up, sending her chair flying. Jack stared up at her in astonishment.

'What are you trying to do, Jack?' she cried. 'Make me admit I love you? You know nothing can come of it—have you simply come here to torture me? Will it give you some sort of sadistic thrill to hear me confess?'

In anguish she clasped her hands together while Jack continued to stare at her in open amazement.

'What in the world are you talking about? Why couldn't anything come of it?' he asked in bewilderment.

She stared down at him incredulously, in that moment both loving and hating him for causing her so much pain.

'For God's sake, Jack,' she whispered, 'do I have to spell it out?'

'Yes, I think maybe you should. . .'

'I would have thought the fact that you have a fiancée might have had something to do with it.'

He continued to stare at her, but the expression in his eyes was indefinable.

At last he let out a long, drawn out sigh. 'Ah, Shakira,' he breathed. Behind him the last orange crescent of the sun slipped below the horizon.

'Yes, Shakira.'

He took a deep breath. 'Shakira and I are no longer engaged,' he said quietly at last.

'What?' She stared at him in amazement.

'We called it off that last night at the Jacaranda Hotel.'

'But. . .but. . . Hilary said. . .'

'Yes,' he raised amused eyebrows, 'what did Hilary say?'

'She said. . .she said. . .the barman had told Paul the pair of you were as good as married. . .then Ruth saw you saying a lingering goodbye. . .' She trailed off, realising just how flimsy was the evidence on which she'd based her assumptions.

He gave a tight little smile. 'A lingering goodbye?' he paused, considering, 'Yes, I suppose it was—our relationship had lasted quite a while really, even if it had been an on-and-off affair most of the time. I'll always be fond of Shakira and I think she will be of me. But in the end we decided to call it a day because it really wasn't going anywhere. Since then I've learnt why it wasn't going anywhere.' He stood up and moved towards her.

'Why?' she breathed, holding her breath.

'Because I wasn't in love with Shakira,' he said quietly. 'Oh, I thought I was, at one time, but I wasn't. I know that now.' He put his hands on her shoulders and stared down into her eyes. 'Besides, it would never have worked. We didn't want the same things out of life. Shakira is a glossy, exotic creature—she loves the luxurious life, the bright lights—I couldn't live like that, any more than I could have expected her to live in the bush. The truth is, Toni, we were totally unsuited—thank God we found out in time. After we parted, I vowed to myself that I wouldn't get involved again for a very long time.' He pulled a face. 'I now know you don't choose the time to fall in love—it chooses you, or rather it simply grabs you by the throat and leaves you helpless.'

As he was speaking he drew her into his arms, and as she rested her head against his chest it felt so familiar, so safe that it was as if she'd reached home after some long, arduous journey.

'Can I dare to hope you might feel the same way?'

he whispered, his voice husky with emotion.

'Oh, Jack, of course you can. I do, oh, I do. . .it was just that I was afraid to let myself love you.'

'I didn't realise you even knew I had been engaged to Shakira, let alone that you thought I still was. You must have thought me a real two-timing rat. . .'

'Now you come to mention it. . .' She gasped as suddenly he pulled her urgently against him then was silenced by his kiss, a kiss that started gently, was full of tenderness, then grew in passion, stirring her own desires and, with his own arousal, promising undreamed-of delights to come.

When they at last drew apart they turned spontaneously towards the view of the valley.

'The sun's gone,' she murmured. 'Do you think it's rising above the waterhole?'

'Probably. We'll go back one day soon for another look.'

'Oh, yes,' she sighed, leaning against him. 'Yes, I want to go back.'

As the dusk gathered around them she gave a sudden shiver.

'You're cold.' He held her closer. 'We can't have that.'

'What do you prescribe, Dr Christy?'

'I have an excellent remedy for restoring body temperature,' he murmured.

'I know,' she answered. 'I remember it well.'

10th

anniversary

Temptation

is Ten!

Join the festivities as Mills & Boon celebrates Temptation's tenth anniversary in February 1995.

There's a whole host of in-book competitions and special offers with some great prizes to be won—watch this space for more details!

In March, we have a sizzling new mini-series Lost Loves about love lost...love found. And, of course, the Temptation range continues to offer you fun, sensual exciting stories all year round.

After ten tempting years, nobody can resist

Temptation **10th**

anniversary

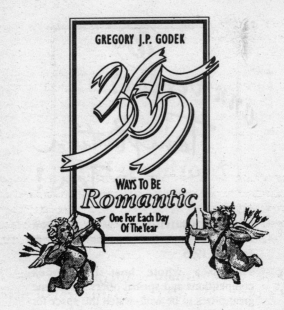
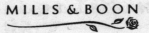

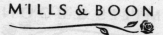

"All it takes is one letter to trigger a romance"

Sealed with a Kiss—**don't miss this exciting new mini-series every month.**

All the stories involve a relationship which develops as a result of a letter being written—we know you'll love these new heart-warming romances.

And to make them easier to identify, all the covers in this series are a passionate pink!

Available now   **Price: £1.90**

MILLS & BOON

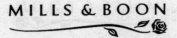

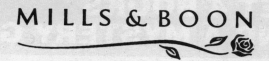

MILLS & BOON

GET 4 BOOKS
AND A MYSTERY GIFT

Return the coupon below and we'll send you 4 Love on Call novels absolutely FREE! We'll even pay the postage and packing for you.

We're making you this offer to introduce you to the benefits of Reader Service: FREE home delivery of brand-new Love on Call novels, at least a month before they are available in the shops, FREE gifts and a monthly Newsletter packed with information.

Accepting these FREE books places you under no obligation to buy, you may cancel at any time, even after receiving just your free shipment. Simply complete the coupon below and send it to:

HARLEQUIN MILLS & BOON, **FREEPOST**, PO BOX 70, CROYDON CR9 9EL.

- -

NO
STAMP
NEEDED

Yes, please send me 4 Love on Call novels and a mystery gift as explained above. Please also reserve a subscription for me. If I decide to subscribe I shall receive 4 superb new titles every month for just £7.20* postage and packing free. I understand that I am under no obligation whatsoever. I may cancel or suspend my subscription at any time simply by writing to you, but the free books and gift will be mine to keep in any case.
I am over 18 years of age.

1EP5D

Ms/Mrs/Miss/Mr _____

Address _____

_____

_____ Postcode _____